STOLEN EMPIRE

BRI BLACKWOOD

BRETAGEY PRESS

Copyright © 2021 by Bri Blackwood

This is a work of fiction. Names, characters, places, and incidents either are the product of the author's imagination or are used fictitiously. Any resemblance to actual persons, living or dead, events, or locales is entirely coincidental. For more information, contact Bri Blackwood.

No part of this book may be reproduced in any form or by any electronic or mechanical means, including information storage and retrieval systems, without written permission from the author, except for the use of brief quotations in a book review.

The subject matter is not appropriate for minors. Please note this novel contains sexual situations, violence, sensitive and offensive language, and dark themes. It also has situations that are dubious and could be triggering.

First Digital Edition: November 2021

Cover Designed by Amanda Walker PA and Design

❃ Created with Vellum

NOTE FROM THE AUTHOR

Hello!

Thank you for taking the time to read this book. Stolen Empire is a dark billionaire romance. It is not recommended for minors because it contains adult situations that are dubious, references to suicide and could be triggering. It is a standalone and the book ends with a happily ever after for our couple.

It would be helpful for you to read Savage Empire, Scarred Empire, Steel Empire, Shadow Empire, and Secret Empire before reading this book. This series is complete. Thank you so much for joining me on this journey!

BLURB

What was stolen...

When my world was ripped out from under me,
  I craved solitude so that I could heal.
  It became a habit until I saw her.
  She might hate me,
  But that's okay.
  She doesn't know that she's my obsession.
  And I'm the only one who can protect her,
  Because she's mine.

PLAYLIST

Mirrors - Justin Timberlake
Without You (feat. Usher) - David Guetta
The Cure - Lady Gaga
Fighter - Christina Aguilera
Scars to Your Beautiful - Alessia Cara
Shallow - Lady Gaga, Bradley Cooper
Beautiful Trauma - P!NK
Mercy - Shawn Mendes
Secret Love Song (feat. Jason Derulo) - Little Mix
I Don't Wanna Live Forever - Taylor Swift, ZAYN
Unconditionally - Katy Perry
Perfect Duet- Ed Sheeran, Beyonce

The playlist can be found on Spotify.

1
KINGSTON

Death.

It was something I had grown used to in this business, but it was still something that could shake you to your core. Loss of human life was something that no one should ever become desensitized to, yet here I was. Staring death in the face and showing no emotion.

Maybe I'd conditioned myself to be used to it at this point.

It felt horrible to lose a person in battle, and I could only imagine how my team would feel. As I stared at Sawyer's cold body, I knew he'd been dead for a while. I hoped the shot to his brain meant that he hadn't suffered much. It would only be a matter of time before the rest of my team was here to clean up the mess.

This one would be harder to clean up. After all, he was one of our own.

Sawyer Maxwell had been a newer member of Cross Sentinel, having been a part of our organization for only a year. He wasn't working on a case at the moment and ended up dead.

He'd been one of our newer recruits and was an excellent team member from what I had been told.

And now he was gone.

With my glove-covered hand, I pulled out a piece of paper that had been placed in the front pocket of his jeans. It was a senseless act, one that could have been avoided. But even before I read what was on the paper, I knew that this murder was directed at me.

I knew who'd killed him.

My father.

Just like he killed my wife.

I'd probably suspected everyone around me at one point or another while grieving. It led to me burying myself in my work and then Cross Sentinel was born. I always wanted to venture out on my own and my wife's death was the catalyst.

I'd failed to protect her. I remember it feeling as if my sanity was on the brink and could snap at any second when I had to identify her body.

In the days after her death, I remember Damien coming to me and trying to be a sounding board because he too knew what it was like to lose someone, even if Damien's ex-girlfriend, Charlotte, wasn't dead.

Although Hayley died years ago now, there was still unfinished business that I needed to take care of, and now I knew it involved the person who was supposed to always be in my corner no matter what.

Not that that meant anything. My father never had my back when I was growing up, so why would he start now?

That didn't mean that I thought he would kill my wife.

I'd kept my distance from my family for a while, including Aunt Selena, who had tried to be a beacon of light during my darkest days. But it wasn't enough. I needed to be by myself to heal.

Heal? That was almost comical because I still couldn't tell anyone if I was healed today.

It'd been seven long years of pain, sacrifice, and anger. Anger about why I couldn't have stopped it from happening.

And the kicker was that my father had organized it all.

My thoughts were brought to a halt when I saw black SUVs flying down the road. In no time, they braked, and members of Cross Sentinel began filing out of the cars one by one.

The dejected looks on their faces were to be expected, but the feelings they must have been experiencing as the result of trying to investigate and clean up the scene were outweighed by one common goal: finding who hurt one of our own.

Although I knew who did it, things were more complicated. Because if I knew my father as well as I thought I did, he wouldn't kill anyone himself. Much like he didn't hurt my uncle or my cousins and their significant others directly. He hired other people to do his dirty work.

"You all right, Boss?"

I nodded at Nick as other members of Cross Sentinel walked around us to investigate Sawyer's body.

"Work with Trish to make sure we have grief counselors ready to go. Whoever wants to see someone, will be able to."

"On it, Boss."

It was the least I could do. After all, it was more than I got as a kid.

My father didn't care how much turmoil he caused or what devastation he left in his wake. All that mattered was him getting what he wanted, no matter the cost. And maybe some of my feelings toward matters such as this came from him.

Well, payback was a bitch, and he should have known that as soon as he did what he did, I would be coming after him, and I wouldn't stop until I achieved my goal: having his head on a platter.

A lot of the puzzle pieces were falling into place. If Uncle Martin knew that my father was responsible for the death of my wife and for trying to cause harm to my cousins, I knew it was because my father wanted him to know. But what else he had up his sleeve would be anyone's guess, and I would do everything to protect anything that was mine.

That meant Eleanor 'Ellie' Winters.

My obsession.

My soon-to-be everything.

"One more. You can give me one more."

I jabbed with my left, pretending that I'm squaring off with someone in the ring instead of hitting the punching bag in front of me. The rush that I got from boxing helped me keep my thoughts from veering too far off course.

"You still got it, Kingston."

I knew he was jokingly taking aim at my age, but I didn't care. I'd known Jae for years and he even worked with me on occasion. Nothing he did or said surprised me anymore.

"Same time next week?"

I nodded. "I'll let you know if that doesn't work for me anymore."

Jae patted me on the shoulder. "Anything you need."

I sensed the underlying meaning to his comment as he walked past me. He knew what date was coming up and attributed my mood to that, but there was a lot more going on that I hadn't told him. Hearing that my father was the one responsible for killing my wife changed everything. I was going to have a conversation with Uncle Martin about it soon, and I wasn't sure how I felt about it. I'd stormed out of the conference room the day he'd revealed his findings, ready to do whatever it took to find my father, but I hadn't been prepared to hear exactly how he'd come to this conclusion. It took a few days for me to gather my thoughts, some that I'd believed had been buried with my dead wife. I thought I'd gotten over a lot of what happened in the circumstances surrounding Hayley's death, but Uncle Martin's news stirred something inside of me that I couldn't explain.

After a quick shower, I walked out to my SUV and sat in the driver's seat, but I couldn't drive away. Not yet.

I pulled out my phone and read a message that confirmed what I thought had happened to Sawyer. The gunshot was what killed him, and he'd been dead for a while. Apparently, he'd been staying in a cabin nearby for a short vacation before he was murdered.

I shook my head as I opened an app that I'd grown fond of over time. I watched as Ellie walked into her apartment before my gaze made its way to the time on my dashboard. *She's home later than usual.*

I watched as she stood in her entryway before kicking the front door closed, her body language telling me that she was lost in thought. The droop of her shoulders told me how tired she was, and part of me wanted to drive over to her place and find ways to ease her tiredness that she felt. But that would all come in due time.

Thankfully, I thought ahead and installed cameras throughout her apartment, convincing myself that I was just being cautious, but I knew that was a lie. It was so I could watch her, immerse myself into her life from afar and think about how that would be enough for me. Us being together would be a disaster and could put her in danger, but I had a hard time staying away. It's because I couldn't. Now, I wondered if I had put her into the crosshairs of my father anyway. Chances were he knew that I was watching her. After all, he taught me many of the things that I knew, including how to spy on a subject.

2

ELLIE

My keys slipped from my fingers and crashed to the floor, and I closed my eyes. I tried to force myself to bend down to pick them up, but even that seemed too hard of a task. Instead, I nudged them with my foot, pushing them farther into the apartment so that I could shut the door behind me.

Home. I was finally home.

After a long day at work, I could have jumped for joy to be back home. I'd been in this apartment since Anais fell in love with Damien and moved out of the apartment that we once shared. It was more than I could have ever dreamed of and not anything that I would have thought to rent if it hadn't been for Damien's generosity and Anais insisting that I move in here. I had to admit it was nice and made my commute easier because this apartment was closer to my job.

I'd taken my time designing my space in an effort to create an at home feel for me. My goal was that whenever I came home, I would be able to not be stressed by the state of my home. It was supposed to be my sanctuary and I took pride in that. The whites and greys that I chose to decorate with further pushed that initiative and was different from how Anais and I decorated our shared apartment together. I sometimes missed having a roommate but having the freedom to do whatever I wanted in my apartment tended to win out and it wasn't like we didn't see each other at all.

Just as I finally convinced myself to bend down and pick up my keys, my phone rang, and I groaned. I didn't feel like talking to anyone tonight, and if I had to guess, it was either a telemarketer or my mother calling.

When I pulled my phone out, I saw it was the latter. I could feel a slight headache forming when I read her name across the screen.

"Hey, I'm just walking in the door. Can you give me a second?"

"Sure. I thought you would have been home by now."

I normally would have, but work had taken longer than usual to wrap up. "Is everything all right?"

"Yes, wanted to call and let you know that Jan has an opportunity—"

I groaned. "Not now."

This came up at least once a month where Mom tried to convince me to pursue another career because she thought I should be making more money. My parents were on the boards of a number of organizations and had connections throughout the city.

"Ellie—"

"Mom, I'm way too old for this conversation that we've had way too many times to count. I enjoy my job and my ability to help people. I'm tired and that's the end of this conversation."

She sighed. "I want the best for you."

"This is what's best for me right now. I enjoy my job, my friends, and my life. If I want to make a switch, I'll let you know. The badgering about my profession has gone on for years and I'm exhausted."

An awkward silence passed between us as I toed off my shoes. My patience was wearing thin.

"How about I call you later?"

"That works. Maybe your father could join us on the call."

That made me smile. "Sure, we can have a party line."

Mom laughed. "Okay and I need to send you an invitation to a fundraiser that we won't be able to attend."

"Sounds good. I'll look out for it."

"Oh and Ellie, take care of yourself, okay? I love you."

I missed my parents. Having to move home for a bit due to my safety being at risk after someone came after Anais gave us the opportunity to spend more time together. I should go and visit them or invite them to NYC one weekend soon.

"Love you, too."

When I ended the call and glanced around my apartment. My eyes landed on my fridge as my stomach growled. Could my headache also be a result of my being hungry? I hurried over to it to see if I could throw something together for dinner. Before I could turn the stovetop on, my phone rang again.

I grinned when I saw whose number appeared on the screen.

"Long time no talk."

"It goes both ways," Anais replied.

It hadn't been a long time since we texted one another pretty regularly.

"What's going on?"

"Nothing much. I have—" Suddenly it occurred to me to tell her of my latest dating adventure, at least what I hoped would be my latest dating adventure. "I think I have a date in a couple of days."

"That's exciting! What do you mean you think you have one?"

"I need to go through my messages on this app, but I'm pretty sure it's for Thursday evening. I can't keep anything straight right now."

"Rough day?"

I sighed. "That's putting it mildly. I also didn't get much sleep last night, so I'm sure that's feeding into how tired I feel."

"Well, I don't want to hold you up, so I'll let you go. Maybe call me after your date."

A light chuckle left my lips. "You just want to be nosy."

"Very true. I'll talk to you later."

"Night."

I hung up and found the dating app I'd started using. I tapped a few buttons and reached the message that contained the details about the date that I was supposed to be going on. I wasn't sure that I wanted to go on the date but felt the need to switch things up. The contents of the messages over the last few days had been above board and hadn't veered into creepy territory thankfully. A drink with an attractive stranger wouldn't be the worst way to spend the evening, or so I hoped.

After confirming the details of the date, I turned my phone on silent. Talking to anyone else was out of the question and if I didn't end up in bed in about twenty minutes, I knew there was a possibility that I would pass out wherever I stood. I flung my phone onto the couch, vowing not to look at it again until the next day, and took a step toward my kitchen. The hairs on the back of my neck rose as my head slowly swerved to the right. An eerie feeling fell over me, and I wasn't sure what to make of it or why it came to be.

You're tired and hungry. I shook off the feeling and walked into my kitchen, determined to find some food and leave the tiring day that I experienced behind me.

Finding something to cook proved to be a challenge, so tossing together some leftovers that I had after several days of takeout was what I ended up with.

I ate my food on my couch while the television played quietly in the background. When I was done, I stood up and walked over to my bookshelf and pulled out a romantic thriller book that I'd ordered online several days ago. I could always start reading this book in the bath.

Determined not to waste another second before cracking the book open, I sank back down into my couch. But before I could open it, I heard something, and I jumped slightly. Goosebumps rose on my skin, and I drew my arms to my chest to rub my hands down them.

What was that? Did I imagine it?

I stood up and walked over to my bookcase which was where I thought I heard the whizzing. Nothing seemed out of the ordinary from how I left it and I didn't hear the noise again.

Chalking it up to me being tired or a bug that I couldn't find anymore, I walked back over to my couch and plopped down on a cushion before I opened the book. Soon I was lost in a world of intrigue, the bath that I'd wanted to take all but forgotten. Thoughts of the noise that I'd heard slipped from my memory as I turned the page on what I hoped was the end of a disastrous day.

3

ELLIE

I walked out the elevator with my head held high, ready to take on whatever the day was about to throw at me. When I walked out the front door of my building, I adjusted the coat that I had on and gasped. I hadn't expected it to be Kingston Cross who was standing in front of me.

"What the hell are you doing here?"

Instead of answering me, Kingston looked me up and down, causing me to roll my eyes.

"I swear you're always where no one wants you to be."

He crossed his arms over his chest and his smile disarmed my annoyance briefly. "For your information, I'm here checking on the feed to make sure that everything is running as it should."

Kingston pointed up, directly at the camera that was facing us. Instead of getting embarrassed that he had a legitimate reason for being here, I shrugged. I had no reason to show him the effect that his smile had on me.

"Is this something I should be concerned about?"

His expression turned serious, and the sudden change shook me. "No."

"Are you lying to me?"

"Why would I do that?"

I scoffed and tucked a piece of my dark hair behind my ear. "Because you like being a dick to me."

A smirk that I'd seen on Damien's face when I'd been in the room with him and Anais, appeared on Kingston's face, and even though they were cousins, the family resemblance was strong. From the neatly kept shortish dark hair and affinity for suits, it was clear that he was a Cross. What made him stand out was his gray eyes, which didn't seem to sparkle. It was as if he kept a ton of secrets behind them and dared for anyone to try to crack his code. I could feel his self-assurance dripping off him, and his gaze never wavered from mine.

"So you're thinking about my dick."

My eyes narrowed. "I liked it better when we didn't talk to one another, especially because this has turned childish. Look, I need to go to work. Go do whatever you...do."

I knew that he owned Cross Sentinel and that he'd helped protect Anais and me when things had gone down with Vincent. I'd be forever grateful for having Nick protect my family and me, but that was it. And I had more important things to do than to talk to him.

My phone dinged in my purse, and when I read the notification I couldn't help but smile.

"What?"

Although I wanted to pretend that I'd forgotten that he was still standing next to me, I couldn't, but he didn't need to know that. My eyes widened and my mouth dropped open as I stared at the screen before I dragged my eyes up to meet

Kingston's. It was the first time I noticed that his eyes were gray. "My date sent me a message confirming where we were meeting tonight."

"Date?" He folded his arms and raised his eyebrow.

"Yeah. You know that thing you do when you want to get to know someone romantically? Date. Listen, I've spent too much time conversing with you and I have things to do."

Without saying anything else, I turned on my heel and walked away. I thought he might try to stop me, but when he didn't, I breathed a sigh of relief. Being around him put me on edge, a feeling that I had a hard time describing other than just being pissed off whenever I was in his presence. I looked down at my phone again and reread the message from Michael before putting it back in my purse. I rolled my shoulders back and continued toward the subway, determined to put my interaction with Kingston behind me.

I FLUFFED my hair and checked myself out in the bathroom mirror. Thankfully, my hair was cooperating today and the light makeup I'd used on my face made a great foundation for turning my day look to something that would be appropriate for evening. I added a brown lipstick that I'd ordered a few months ago to my lips, choosing something different than my normal look. Not that it would change my attitude; I pretty much made it through life by causing shit and asking questions later. The lipstick reflected my personality better.

I grabbed my large purse that I'd brought with me so that I'd have enough room to pack my uniform and walked out of the door.

"Have a good evening," I said as I walked past Jill. "You too!"

Her cheerfulness at this time of evening was contagious and I looked over my shoulder to wave at her as I exited the building. I walked down the street, but instead of focusing on the first date I'd been on in a while, I couldn't take my mind off of my encounter with Kingston.

I hopped on the subway and rode a couple of stops to get to my destination. Bar 53 was a fancy bar that had only been open for a couple of years. In my opinion, it was a perfect place for a first date, and I was happy that we decided to go here. The vibe of the bar was mellow, the perfect place to give two strangers the opportunity to get to know one another. The soft rock playing in the background was the cherry on top for this stunning atmosphere that I hoped would lead to a date that would at least be fun if not something more.

I used to have no problem dating, but it hadn't interested me in a while. Instead, I took the time to focus on myself. By the time I would have dipped my foot into the dating pond again, danger had come knocking and Anais was in trouble while I went to stay with my parents in New Jersey with a bodyguard.

It didn't take me long to find Michael, who I was thankful looked like his profile photo. Maybe this wasn't a bad idea after all. As I approached the table, he stood up and I gave him a once-over. He hadn't lied about his height either if my estimations were correct.

"You look even more stunning in person," he said when I walked up to the table.

I smiled at his compliment, happy that it seemed that this date was getting off on the right foot.

Thoughts of this date going well crashed and burned as soon as we received our drinks that we'd ordered.

"My life at work has turned into hell."

When the conversation continued to devolve into more about his accounting job, I tuned him out, instead choosing to stare at my drink. I had no issue with him talking about his profession, but as I waited for him to ask me something about me, the topic never shifted, so I was left hearing him complain about work for what felt like an eternity. I wished that it was more potent, then maybe it wouldn't make this date seem so unbearable. But ordering another meant that I would have to stay here longer. Decisions...decisions...

A yawn left my lips, and I quickly covered my mouth, hoping not to appear rude. Michael stopped mid-sentence. "Is everything okay?"

A fake smile appeared on my lips. "Ah, yes. I'm sorry. I had a long day at work and my tiredness took over."

"Can we wrap this up and meet up again sometime soon? Maybe on a day when neither one of us has to work? I've had a great time talking to you and don't want to let that go."

It's because I haven't been able to get a word in. "Sure, that would be great." The lie fell from my tongue with ease.

When he got the attention of the waiter and pulled at his wallet to pay the bill, I took a bigger sip of my drink. The vibe of the bar was excellent during the short time I'd been here, and I made a note to return, even if it wouldn't be with him.

While he took care of the check, I stood up and put my coat on and pushed in my chair. As I waited for him to wrap up things, I counted down the seconds until I would be back in my apartment, with my sweatpants on and vegging in front of the television.

When he had his things, we walked toward the exit. I decided quickly that I would take a taxi back home, because I didn't want to deal with any awkwardness that might result if he had been planning on taking the subway. As if someone was hearing my pleas, a taxi was about to drive past the bar, and my hand shot up to flag the driver down.

"Well, this is me." I walked toward the taxi, which was double-parked and blocking oncoming traffic.

"I had a lovely evening with you, Ellie."

I nodded and when he opened his arms as if he was going to hug me, that same hand fell back down, landed in front of us, and welcomed a handshake from him.

When he placed his hand in mine, I said, "It was nice meeting you."

Before he could hold me up anymore, I opened the taxi door and slid into my seat. He closed the door behind me, and I gave him a small wave as he backed away from the car and the taxi sped off. It was then I let out a deep breath. He hadn't asked for my number, so the likelihood of him reaching out to me again was slim. I pulled out my phone and debated blocking him on the dating app but decided against it. If he messaged me again, I would tell him that I didn't think we were a good fit. I ended up sending a quick text to Anais before I put my phone away.

Me: *Tonight's date was a bust. Happy I went though.*
Anais: *I'm sorry it didn't work out.*
Me: *It's fine. I'm going to go home and relax.*
Anais: *Let's get dinner together this week?*
Me: *Perfect.*

"Are you fucking kidding me?" I mumbled under my breath as I crossed my arms over my chest. Why was Kingston in the lobby of my apartment building at this time of the evening?

Please don't see me. Please don't see me. I picked up the pace and walked toward the elevators, hoping that Kingston wouldn't spot me. Chances of that were nil given how empty the lobby was and because he was only looking down at whatever that was on the screen in front of him. He was sitting behind the front desk. As if he knew I was staring, he looked up, and when his eyes met mine, I did my best to control the tremble that threatened to flow through my body. I was willing to say that I thought he was attractive, but that didn't mean I wouldn't take an opportunity to punch him in the face. I turned my head to focus on the elevators that would take me up to my place and away from him.

I hoped that there was an elevator waiting, but it was just my luck that there wasn't, so I pressed the button and took a step back.

"Ellie."

I jumped before my eyes slammed shut. I hadn't heard him walk up behind. The marble floor in the lobby made it easy to hear footsteps, but Kingston had somehow avoided making any sound. I took a deep breath before I turned around to face him.

"Have fun on your date? I didn't expect you'd be back so soon."

Involuntarily, I clenched my fist. "That is none of your business." My annoyance blinded me for a moment before I followed up with, "Why would you be expecting me at all?"

"You don't know how wrong that statement is."

What was that supposed to mean? And it didn't go unnoticed that he had ignored my question. "What the hell are—"

"Have a good night, Ellie." As quickly as Kingston had come up behind me, he left. He didn't bother stopping at the front desk, instead walking to the front doors and out into the streets of New York City.

The dinging of the elevator caused me to jump again, and when the doors opened, I rushed inside and repeatedly pressed the button that would close them again.

The trip up to my apartment was uneventful and once I closed my front door behind me, shutting him out of my life, only then could I breathe.

4

KINGSTON

The door closed softly behind, the light from the hallway a thing of the past. Darkness surrounded me and that was what I preferred.

I had one mission and one mission alone: to fix the camera that I'd placed in Ellie's apartment.

Now was the perfect opportunity to do it, since Anais had invited Ellie over to her and Damien's larger home for dinner. It gave me ample time to do what I needed to do.

The camera was tiny, but when Ellie had replaced one of the books on her shelf, she shifted the camera, and the angle was now askew. I pulled out my phone to use as a flashlight and walked over to the bookcase. I quickly fixed the camera and took a step back.

The light from my flashlight danced around the room, allowing me to see if anything was out of place. Seeing nothing, I glanced at the room that seemed to be calling my name and decided that a more thorough review of her apartment was required. The first place I walked into was her bedroom.

I'd put a camera near a small potted plant on a floating

shelf she had attached to the wall. The camera pointed directly at her bed, and I wouldn't deny that I fully embraced how lucky I was that she chose to decorate the apartment this way. Thankfully, she also didn't tend to adjust the plant up there so the camera was safe for the time being.

Although I usually kept my viewings to when she was in the living room, I'd also take an opportunity to look at her while she slept. The feistiness that she displayed for the world was gone in the blink of an eye once her eyes drifted closed and her breathing evened out. She looked so at peace, a complete one-eighty from how she looked when she was near me. But that would change, I was sure of it.

The camera had also given me insight into her dating habits or lack thereof since she moved into this building. She hadn't brought anyone to the apartment as most of the dates that she had been on didn't make it past date number one. That all would change too.

Because there would be no one else.

I checked my watch, noting that I had just a few minutes before I needed to get out of there. I had an important meeting, and I didn't want Ellie to find me in her apartment. I should have left as quickly as I entered, but when my arm brushed against the dresser as I was heading toward the door, I couldn't help myself. I stopped and opened the top drawer and found some pieces of lingerie.

My fingers touched the lace and I imagined what it would look like on her. The tough exterior that she liked to show whenever I was near loved the feel of softer fabrics against her skin. I made a mental note about it before closing the drawer.

I quickly left the room, refusing to get distracted again.

After all I had one mission, but it didn't hurt to double-check everything and to make sure that the apartment was as safe as I left it the last time I was in here. I made my way around, checking for any security threats, and once I verified that everything was as safe as it could be, I exited her apartment just as quietly as I had come in and I knew she would be none the wiser.

"Kingston?"

I cracked a small smile as I stepped into my aunt's arms. A stark reminder of how she'd embraced me the moment when I'd gotten the worst news of my life...twice.

"I wasn't expecting you this evening."

"I know. Uncle Martin asked that I come and talk to him about twenty minutes ago."

"He didn't mention that..." Her eyes widened as if she'd realized what this visit could be about. She brought me back into her arms, gently patting my back. She pulled away and I studied my face. "Do you want me to come in there with you?"

What Uncle Martin was about to tell me must have been brutal. A flash of a memory reminded me of how she'd tried to help me pick up all of the pieces when I'd ended up on her doorstep as I got the news that would change my life forever.

I shook my head. "This is something that I need to deal with on my own, but I'll make sure I say goodbye before I leave here, no matter what."

The small smile Aunt Selena gave me was full of encouragement. She grabbed my hand with both of hers and squeezed. "You know we are here for you no matter what."

I know."

"You know the way to Martin's office," she said as she moved aside.

"Uncle Martin," I said as I knocked on the door to his office in his place in the city. I opened the door and found him sitting behind his desk, writing something down on a notepad in front of him. He looked up as I walked inside, and I closed the door behind me.

"Take a seat," he said and gestured to the chair in front of his desk. This office was designed similarly to the one at the Cross estates. The darker colors and wooden details brought back memories of my childhood and when Mom would take me to visit my cousins. Before my world was upended. "I'm glad you're willing to talk about this."

"If it means putting an end to all of this shit, you know I would have done it. No matter how much trauma it brings up for me. I'm sorry I stormed out of the conference room a few days ago."

"Given what I said, I completely understand why." The grim look on Uncle Martin's face had to mirror mine. I was sure of it.

"Why do you think my father is behind all of this?"

Uncle Martin ran a hand through his hair, which seemed to be growing grayer by the minute. "Because Neil sent me these things."

He picked up an envelope and handed it to me. I stared at it before I pulled out its contents. I looked down at the item in my hand and back up at Uncle Martin. "It's a couple of photos that have part of them burned off."

Uncle Martin pushed back from his desk and stood up. With his hands resting behind his back, one hand in the other, he walked over to one of the windows overlooking New York's skyline. His silence was deafening.

I looked back down at the photo, taking my time to study it. It was an older photo, and I recognized my grandfather. In the photo, he looked to be close to my age, and soon my eyes made their way to the boy standing next to him. "This one looks like a photo of Granddad and my father."

"It is. It was a photo of all three of us before your father burnt the other end, removing me from it. Turn it over and read the back."

I did as he said. "The fun has only just begun."

I examined the other photo, which was newer by comparison. I recognized it and could feel anger growing in my belly. It had been a photo of me as a baby, my mother and him and now the only one that was left in it was him.

"Not many people know about what we've been dealing with, but I don't think it was a coincidence that he used fire to remove me from the photo. After all what happened with Damien and Charlotte..."

I nodded, understanding what he was getting at. "He's using this as a warning to you that he wants you out of the way."

He turned around and looked me dead in the eye. "And by extension my sons, which includes you."

I put the photo back on Uncle Martin's desk. "And you're sure he sent it?"

Uncle Martin raised an eyebrow. "I know my brother better than anyone, and he's the only one who would have had access to this photo. Neil is smart. Always has been, but he constantly lets one thing get in his way: jealousy."

"What do you mean including me?"

"You became a target the moment I brought you to the Cross estates after your mother was killed. I took his only heir and brought him into my home instead of letting you fend for yourself. I suspected that he would come back and try something, but after years of silence on his end, even when I tried to reach out to him, I thought he had given up. I was wrong."

"But you told me years ago that you gave him enough money to disappear."

Uncle Martin walked back over to his desk and placed his hands on the surface. "Sometimes hatred goes deeper than money, and no amount could pay off how much your father hates that he has had to face the consequences of his actions. This is his way of attacking us all although his focus is primarily on me and you."

"You mean because Granddad didn't leave him anything related to Cross Industries. I always assumed he hated me for being born."

He nodded. "Even though he was his first born. My father knew well enough that there was no way that Neil would be able to carry on his legacy and keep Cross Industries afloat. He explained this to Neil long before he passed away, but of course Neil was convinced that I'd had something to do with it even though my father left plenty of money and other resources for him to support himself. He's hated me since then and that hatred only increased after I stepped in with you."

"But he didn't fight you at all when you came to get me. In

fact I vividly remember him telling you to 'get this piece of shit out of my sight.' It almost broke me even though we've never had the best relationship."

Uncle Martin walked around his desk and placed a hand on my shoulder. "I wish you'd never heard that. Your mother did all she could do to protect you from his wrath, and I did what I could from the sidelines, and when she left this Earth, I knew it was only a matter of time before he really turned on you. So I stepped in."

I looked up at him standing over me, much like he'd done for most of my life. "And I'll never be able to thank you enough for doing that."

He nodded before clearing his throat. "So you see why it's dire that we find him and put an end to this. He's tried to find a way to destroy us, and he won't stop until he does."

"I do." I started thinking of how my team could aid in finding my father before Uncle Martin spoke again.

"I have my suspicions that he had something to do with what happened to Hayley as well."

"I'll find out for sure."

Digging up what happened to Hayley wasn't something that I wanted to think about right now because I knew it would send me on a downward spiral. My focus needed to be on finding my father, before he did something else that would hurt someone I cared about.

"What's this I hear about you and Anais's best friend?"

Ellie. Her name floated through my mind as I thought back to seeing her yesterday and how I'd set it up. I knew when she left her apartment to go to work, around what time she returned, and spent a lot of my free time watching her while she was in her apartment. Hell, even when I was working, I'd sometimes have her video feed on in the background and glance at it every once in a while to see what she was doing.

I watched her while she was on a date with the asshole she met on a dating app. It was clear that the date hadn't gone well because of how quickly she left the bar.

Because I watched her.

Her every move.

I knew what she was thinking before she thought it. And was ready to use all of that to my advantage.

"Kingston."

I turned to look at my uncle. I wasn't about to admit that he'd caught me lost in my thoughts about Ellie.

"Yes?"

Uncle Martin smiled for the first time since I'd arrived. "Damien mentioned that something might be going on there. I would be careful with her."

"What do you mean—?"

"This has nothing to do with you as a person. I'm worried that Neil will stop at nothing to make sure that he tears down the people who he thinks have wronged him, and if he suspects that you might have a weak spot there, well…"

Uncle Martin didn't have to spell it out and I knew that he was right. I thought back to how Carter, someone who I entrusted with my cousin's fiancée's life, ended up being a traitor. I made sure that there was another extensive background check done on everyone else who worked for Cross Sentinel, but there was still always the chance that someone or something might slip through the cracks no matter how much you might be prepared.

"I understand."

"Good. If I hear anything else, I'll let you know."

I stood up and gave him a hug. "Same goes with me."

"We're going to get him."

"I know."

I walked to the door and opened it with Uncle Martin following behind me. I stopped in the living room and gave Aunt Selena a hug, keeping my promise, and soon I was back in my SUV, preparing to pull out of my parking spot.

What kept replaying in my head were the things he said about Ellie and Hayley. One was gone long ago, and I made a vow to avenge her death. The other was very much alive and I would stop at nothing to keep her safe, even if she couldn't stand the sight of me.

That was all going to change.

I'd kept mostly to myself when it came to her, remaining in the background while she lived her life.

And that time was coming to an end.

I checked my phone to see if I'd gotten any messages and found one from Damien.

Damien: *Everything is ready to go. Stop by my office on Monday morning so that we can set everything in motion.*

Perfect.

The deal had gone through. I needed to thank Damien for pulling some strings so I could make this purchase, forcing another piece to fall into place as I got closer to making my move.

5
ELLIE

There was no doubt in my mind that I could fall asleep standing up right now if given the chance. Another long day at Devotional Spa was starting to feel like a recurring nightmare. Due to an influx of patrons and us losing a couple members of our team, the rest of us needed to pick up the slack in order to make sure that everyone received their proper treatment, usually from pain.

All I could think about was walking to my apartment, taking off my clothes, and rolling into bed. I didn't know if I even had enough strength to pull together a quick dinner. That might have to be something that I did after I rested my weary body for a couple of hours.

I looked up and noticed that I was only a couple of blocks away from my place. I felt a small surge of energy pass through me, and I assumed my body was trying to quicken the pace and get home as fast as possible. All that came to a grinding halt when a man stepped in front of me.

I sidestepped the person but when they followed my lead, blocking me once again, I knew things weren't quite as they seemed. Before I could react again, someone grabbed me, dragging me into a nearby alleyway that I had walked past.

As I was about to scream, his hand clamped down on my mouth. I could feel him tugging at my purse and fight or flight instinct kicked in.

It might not have been the smartest thing I've ever done, but something in my brain told me that I should try everything possible to stop this robber. Instead of letting go of the purse, I held on and managed to wrangle myself free from his grip.

I turned to look over my shoulder briefly to see if someone was a witness to what had happened before I yelled, "Get off my purse, you asshole! Someone help!"

Suddenly, I let the purse go. Fear ran down my spine as I looked at the knife in front of me. I could see the light flickering off of its silver blade. I put my hands up and took a step back, hoping that I hadn't pissed off the assailant enough that he was willing to stab me. As I took another deep breath to scream once more, a noise behind me scared us both.

"Get away from her."

Before I could react, the man shoved me hard and ran. I ended up hitting the brick wall behind me. I glanced to my left and saw a rusty pointed pole sticking out of the wall. A couple of inches to the left and I was convinced that I knew I would have been impaled on it.

"Are you okay?" I turned and found Kingston standing there. He bent down, picked up a piece of paper, and stuffed it into his pocket.

I slowly nodded my head as I tried to find the words to say. Never in a million years would I have been thankful to see him in this dark alleyway in the middle of New York City.

"I'm fine, but he stole my purse."

"Don't worry about that. It's more important that you're okay."

His long stride ate up the distance between us and soon he grabbed my forearms, examining me as if trying to see if I was telling the truth about being okay.

"You aren't fine. Whoever did this cut you." Kingston's words were barely above a growl.

I looked down and confirmed that he had. I didn't feel any pain from it because I'd been so focused on being impaled on the wall. Kingston pulled out a handkerchief and put it on the wound.

"I doubt I need stitches," I said. I glanced at the pole that was almost taunting me at this point. "This could have ended a lot differently."

Kingston followed my gaze and pulled me off the wall. "We won't think about that. Let me get you back to your apartment. We need a first aid kit and I'll patch you up when we get back to your place." He placed his arm around my shoulders, helping to steady me. I hesitated before wrapping my arm around his waist as we started the short trek to my apartment. He pulled out his phone and quickly typed something into it using his thumb.

"I should file a police report."

This time he hesitated, before he put his phone back in his pocket and glanced at me. "We can discuss that when we get you home."

Not having the energy to argue with him, we quietly slipped through the front doors of my apartment building a few minutes later and he whisked me up into the elevator. When he pressed the button that would drop us off at my floor, I looked up at him and raised an eyebrow. How had he known which floor I lived on?

"Nick," he said, answering my question with one word.

That made sense. Nick had been assigned to me when Anais was in danger, for fear that whoever was after her would come after me. I remembered that when things had settled down and both Anais and I had officially moved out of our old apartment, Nick had stopped by to make sure things were safe and sound in my new place.

On the other hand, it had been a while ago. When had Nick checked in with Kingston about where I lived? I thought about questioning him further, but there were more important matters that needed to be settled. "I don't have a key to my apartment. It was in my purse."

I could see the gears turning in Kingston's head. Before he could respond, the elevator announced its arrival to my floor and a woman I'd never seen before appeared. She gave a small smile to both me and Kingston before she walked past us and opened my front door. She then turned and handed the key to me.

"If you need anything else, please let me know."

Without waiting for us to reply, she walked away, vanishing as quickly as she appeared.

I turned to Kingston, who said, "I texted the front desk before we arrived and had them get a copy of your key."

I dipped my head, happy that he had the clarity to figure out a way for us to open the front door. Kingston closed the door behind us and walked with me over to my couch. Before I could sit down, he started unbuttoning my coat.

"I can undo it myself, thanks," I said sarcastically.

Kingston's face remained stoic as he watched me ease the

coat off my shoulders. There was still some lingering pain from being slammed against a brick wall, but it could have been worse.

I lowered myself down onto the couch and groaned. "I need to call the police and cancel my credit cards. This is going to be a pain in the ass."

Kingston said nothing, but he took a step back and scanned my apartment with his eyes. Instead of interrupting him, I watched in amazement as he seemed to be double-checking my apartment; for what I didn't know. When he was done he pulled out his phone and gave it his full attention. Questions grew in my mind as his fingers flew across the screen. When I'd had enough, I cleared my throat and his attention shifted back to me.

"Where is your first aid kit?"

"Bathroom. In the cabinet under the sink."

Kingston's long stride allowed him to easily make it to my bathroom and back before I could blink. I watched as he cleaned my wound and bandaged it up. Once he neatly put everything back in the kit, he stopped moving and pulled out his phone.

"What's going on? Can I use your phone to make a few phone calls?" Given the situation, since I asked nicely, there was no way he could say no, right?

Instead of answering me, he held up his index finger, signaling for me to remain quiet. A few seconds later, there was a knock on the door of my apartment, and Kingston walked to the door and opened it. He thanked the person at the door and shut it. I watched as he put something in his pocket before he turned his body toward me. Before I could ask him what he stuffed in his pocket, I saw that he had my purse in hand.

"You found it!" I almost jumped up from my seat on the couch, but my body warned me not to move too quickly after what I had just been through. Kingston glared at me as he could see that I was about to jump up in my excitement, stopping me in my tracks.

"Ellie, you need to rest. I don't think that there were any injuries outside of the cut and some potential soreness when the adrenaline wears off, but it doesn't mean you should be jumping up and down."

I started to argue with him but bit my tongue when he handed me my purse. I quickly shifted through the contents and found that everything was still there.

"Anything missing?"

I shook my head. "Nope, everything is where it should be. Where was it found?"

He glanced down at his phone and then said, "Seems as if the robber tossed it before he scaled a fence in an attempt to get away. Several of my men are searching for him right now."

"I still need to cancel these credit cards, just in case."

"Makes sense."

I looked back at Kingston and his expression hadn't changed. My gaze didn't shift from him until I felt my phone vibrating in my purse. I pulled it out and found a familiar name displayed on the screen. At least it was still working.

"Hey."

"Hey yourself. Is everything all right? Kingston sent Damien a text about what happened."

Anais's elevated voice caused me to panic slightly even though I wasn't hurt.

"I'm fine. Currently sitting in my apartment."

"Is Kingston still there?" I could hear Anais shuffling on the other end of the line. Her voice was then muffled as if she was talking to someone else close to her.

"He is. He handed me my purse. Someone found it."

"Thank goodness. Damien and I will be at your place shortly."

"Oh, you guys don't have to come. I'll be okay." There was absolutely no reason for either one of them to stop by. I wasn't really injured and I had my purse back. Sure, I still felt violated due to the audacity of someone stealing my personal belongings, but there was no way that anyone would be able to help me get over it. It was something that I hoped to move past on my own... eventually.

"You were there for me at one of the lowest moments of my life. How could I not be there for you during a time like this? I'm also happy to stay with you, if that's helpful. It's the least I can do."

I heard some more words being exchanged between Anais and who I assumed was Damien before she said, "Ellie, we should be there shortly. See you soon."

She ended the call before I could reply. I placed my phone next to my purse and dropped my head in my hands. A headache was forming, and I wasn't sure if it was due to me being thrown against a wall or having to deal with this period.

Kingston said nothing as I squeezed the bridge of my nose, hoping to relieve some of the pressure. I was thankful for the silence because that meant I didn't have to say anything to him. I knew I should relay Anais's message, but even that seemed like a huge feat now. My mind jumped to the knife-wielding mugger and how if things had taken a turn, I could have easily been injured or killed. I know at times like these you should look at the bright side, but the bright side seemed further and further away.

I moved my hands from my face and turned to find Kingston staring at me. His arms were crossed over his wide chest, displaying power and strength during a time like this. His gaze remained unflinching, even though I had caught him in the act. It was as if he wanted me to know that he was studying my every move instead of shifting his eyes to focus on something else.

"I think I need to take a shower," I announced. "I'm hoping that might help me relax."

"Do you need any help with that?"

I was taken aback by his suggestion, and I knew that what I was thinking was written all over my face. Yet he looked on unapologetically, not giving a damn about how his words sounded.

"I think I can manage. After all, I've been bathing myself for thirty plus years."

The corner of his mouth twitched, indicating that my comment had the desired effect. I eased up off the couch and walked to the bathroom. The desire to turn around and look back to see what Kingston was doing was there. I told myself it was due to having him in my apartment and still being shaken up from the incident. Not only had I been assaulted and robbed, Kingston had switched from being someone I viewed as a pain in the ass into a hero. If he hadn't been there, I don't know what...

Wait? How had he been there? Was it by chance that he had been doing some work at my apartment building that led him to being in the right place at the right time? That was plausible because he was in this building a lot. The thoughts that were coming to my mind were starting to make my headache worse. I pushed them to the side as I turned on the showerhead and sighed. When I started to remove my clothes, I began to feel a tenderness in my back that I knew was due to being slammed against the wall. It made it a little more difficult to get undressed, but I managed. There was no way in hell that I was going to call Kingston to help me anyway, so I needed to manage it on my own.

When I stepped into the shower and the hot water cascaded over my body, I sighed again. One would have thought that I would start crying, but somehow, I held it together. After all, I was home, safe in my apartment even if I had someone who was a practical stranger just a couple rooms over. I hated to admit it but having him here made me feel safer. We might not see eye to eye, and he was a total prick when we first met, but I knew that he wouldn't let anyone harm me.

Yet the way he stared at me caused a sensation that I couldn't quite describe. It was as if he was looking into my soul and taking note of every crack and crevice he could find. It was unnerving because I had no idea how to read him. It didn't seem fair that he had that ability, or maybe I was imagining it, but there wasn't anything I could do about it now.

Instead, I focused on trying to clear my mind. A nice glass of wine would do wonders as well.

I took my time finishing my shower and although there was still some soreness, I felt almost brand-new when I stepped onto my bathmat. There were a couple things I could do to potentially help ease some of the tightness that I was feeling.

"Wrap yourself up in a blanket. It's chilly here and you're cold."

I couldn't help but roll my eyes and looked down at the sweatpants and shirt that I'd put on when I exited the shower. "Are you intentionally trying to piss me off?"

"No."

"Then leave me alone."

"You just shivered. I know what you need right now and you're trying to show how strong you are. Stop fighting me for one second and do it."

"Kingston, cut out the bossy, macho shit. Now is not the time for you to act as if you give a damn."

"You like painting this picture that nothing is wrong when you're frightened out of your mind, don't you?"

I kept my expression neutral because I hated that he knew how I felt. "I don't have time for your psychoanalytical crap either."

I was saved from having to listen to his answer by the doorbell. Instead of spewing something that would contradict me again, he did the most helpful thing he could do given the circumstances: opened the front door.

Before Kingston could open it fully, Anais burst into the hallway and headed straight toward me, her arms stretched out in front of her. She pulled me into a hug.

"Are you okay?"

I nodded, too overcome with emotion to voice my words.

"I know what you felt," Anais whispered in my ear as she rubbed a hand up and down my back.

There wasn't anything that could stop the tears from flow-ing. She understood how I felt when she was kidnapped, and we were all worried about whether she would be alive when she was found. I didn't even want to think about that again.

My eyes snapped shut trying to hold my emotions back, but it was fruitless. I didn't bother wiping the tears away because it meant breaking my hug with Anais and it felt good to cry.

When my eyes slowly opened, I found Damien and Kingston talking to one another near my kitchen counter. Although Kingston was the one doing the talking, his eyes were trained on me. An unsettling feeling sat in my stomach as neither one of us broke eye contact with the other. Anais pulled back, freeing me from her grasp, and examined my face. That was when I finally looked away from the man who had saved me from potentially getting more bruised or battered tonight. Or worse, killed.

Anais grabbed some tissues out of her pocket and handed them to me, helping me dry my face. When we finished, she looked down at my bandage before her eyes bounced between me and the two men talking quietly across the room.

"You know," Anais said, turning her face to me, "maybe it wouldn't hurt to have Kingston here for a couple of days..."

I was taken aback that Anais would think up this ridiculous plan. "It was a robbery. The dude is probably long gone by now."

"Yeah, but he didn't find what he was looking for clearly, if all your possessions were returned. He didn't even take your cash."

"I know. It wasn't much but it was an easy steal so I'm not sure why he didn't."

Anais put her hand on my knee and said, "Having

Kingston stay the night and us upstairs should hopefully calm your nerves. Anyone in this situation would be a nervous wreck right now."

I looked at everyone in the room and could tell that although they were silent, all three agreed with this stance. Having someone here with me wouldn't be the worst thing in the world, in case whoever did this came back. Now, they might be able to find out where I lived but would they be expecting Kingston to be here? Besides the fact that the security in the building was top-notch, I always believed that there were ways to break into the most secure places.

"Fine, but he has to sleep on the couch."

Anais raised an eyebrow. "You have a guest bedroom though?"

"And I wasn't expecting a guest. There's so much crap in that room right now that I don't even want to talk about it."

6

ELLIE

I woke up the next morning and silence greeted me. Being able to sleep in was lovely and I felt fortunate that I had the day off.

If I hadn't, I would have taken off of work because there was no way I would have been able to do my job and be on my feet for long periods of time. A small stretch proved that my back and neck were still sore, but I expected that by the time the adrenaline fully wore off, I'd feel worse. I moved slowly getting out of bed and paused with one leg over the side.

It had just clicked that I'd allowed Kingston to stay over and that there was a good chance that he was still sleeping on my couch. Dread about facing him creeped to the surface of my subconscious before I could tamp it down. Why was I growing nervous about him being here? If he pissed me off, which there was a high chance of him doing, I had no problem kicking him out.

Once the covers were fully off my body, I shivered slightly because of the coolness in the air. I'd replaced my clothes from last night with a tank top and shorts and was regretting that decision now.

I walked into the master bathroom that was adjacent to my bedroom and threw on a fluffy black bathrobe that reached my knees. I also found myself checking my hair out in the mirror and making sure I looked presentable before I walked back through my bedroom and into the living area where I was almost sure to find Kingston.

When I left my bedroom, silence greeted me, and when my eyes landed on the couch, I could see why. I saw the top of Kingston's head, an arm, and his foot propped up on the arm of the couch. The blanket that I had given him last night was covering the rest of his body. I was shocked that he wasn't awake since I painted him as someone who got up at the crack of dawn ready to start his day and annoy anyone and everyone. I slowly made my way into the living room, being sure to be quiet so I didn't disturb him.

I tiptoed over toward the couch and found him with an arm under the pillow, and an arm across his torso, and the blanket sitting low on his waist, exposing his entire chest to me. Given how cool it was this morning, I wondered if it made sense to walk over there and pull the blanket up, so he didn't feel cold.

Where had that thought come from?

That idea quickly left my mind because everything happened in the blink of an eye. The next thing I knew, I was staring down the barrel of Kingston's gun. My hands shot up in defense, to show him that I wasn't armed, and I couldn't even fix myself to scream. Who the hell slept with a gun under their pillow?

"Fuck," Kingston mumbled as he lowered his weapon.

"Tell me how you really feel about me," I said, gesturing to the gun once he'd lowered it.

"You have no idea," he said as he stared me down.

The look he gave me was smoldering and made me want to melt into a puddle where I stood. Although there was no way he could see them through the thick bathrobe I had on, I crossed my arms to hide my chest, due to the tingling I felt in my breasts. It annoyed me that I couldn't stand him for all these months and now with just one look, I was turning into putty in his hands. The shift in emotions that I had from having a gun pulled on me to his hot smoldering gaze was like a whiplash. My brain chalked it up to him saving me the evening before.

"Any updates from last night?"

"Not really."

"Not even about the paper that you picked up? I saw you put it into your pocket last night."

His eyes widened slightly before returning to his normal passive expression. I was grateful that the heated look in his eye was gone because it felt as if I could breathe again. "I didn't know you saw me do that."

"I'm more observant than you think, clearly."

"That's obvious."

"So will you tell me about the piece of paper or am I going to have to ask you again?"

I could see the debate waging a war within him. Instead of responding, he threw the blanket to the side and stood up, giving me a full view of his body. A few tattoos lined his chest, and I couldn't help but stare. I wanted to know their story and why he'd chosen them, but I also knew that I had no right to it.

What I did have a right to know was what he picked up from the scene of my attack and if it was somehow related to catching whoever had attacked me.

"It was a piece of paper."

I waited for him to continue, and when he didn't, I grew frustrated. "Tell me everything. I have a right to know."

Instead of saying something else, he reached over and grabbed the pants that he'd on the night before. I couldn't help but watch as the muscles in his arm flexed with every move that he made. He pulled out the piece of paper and leaned over to hand it to me. I stared at the scrap of paper hanging between his index and middle fingers before I snatched it out of his hand. My eyes made their way back to his and then looked down to read what was in my hand.

My mouth opened slightly as I read and then read it again.

"It has my address, and someone wrote down the time frame 6:15 p.m. to 8:15 p.m." I said it more out loud to myself than to Kingston, who I knew already had this information. "Wait, that's usually around the time I've gotten home recently."

"I thought as much. Which means we have an even bigger problem here."

I didn't reply right away, and when it clicked, it shook me to my core. "What happened last night wasn't random, was it?"

Kingston shook his head, confirming a big fear of mine. Yes, having someone violate you in any way was horrible, but I had assumed that the attack had been random. If this pointed to the assumption that both Kingston and I reached, that concerned me.

Someone had it out for me, and I had no idea who. "Maybe we should go to the police with this. Much like I wanted to do last night."

"And what are they going to do about any of this?" Irritation and warning were laced in his voice. Yet, I didn't heed any of it.

"I don't know, but it wouldn't hurt to have them looking into what happened."

"Are you so sure about that?"

His words made me freeze in place. What was he keeping from me?

"There's plenty of things that you don't know."

"Why don't you enlighten me, then?"

The energy in the room was frosty at best, arctic cold at worst.

"The less you know the better."

"You aren't going to disrespect me, especially not in my own home, Kingston."

Kingston took a step toward me, closing the gap between us. My glare was fixated on him, daring him to do something. If he was smart and wanted to live, he'd stop while he was ahead.

He didn't give a fuck.

"My goal is to keep you alive and unharmed by any means necessary. If that means I have to keep things that might further cause you harm to myself then so be it."

"And if I tell you to get the fuck out of my place?"

"Then you're at the mercy of whoever is trying to harm you. Do you think they wanted to just steal your purse? They didn't take the cash that was easy to grab."

His words bounced off of every wall in my apartment as

his stare burned through me. I didn't have a response for him, and I knew he had me right where he wanted me. Instead, I turned on my heel and walked over to my fridge to pour a glass of orange juice.

"Have we reached an agreement?"

I froze at his comment, my hand still holding on to the glass bottle in the fridge. I hadn't heard him follow me into the kitchen, and I suspected that was the effect he wanted.

"An agreement about what?"

"Are you going to kick me out or am I going to protect you? The choice is yours."

The look in his eyes dared me to choose the incorrect answer. What choice did I actually have here? I could either have Kingston help me or spend the rest of my life looking over my shoulder wondering if this was the day I was going to get hurt, or worse.

I put the orange juice bottle on the countertop and closed the refrigerator door. "What exactly is it that you will do?"

"It would be similar to what we did last time around. For you when Anais was in trouble."

"Should my parents be put under surveillance again?"

"We have no inclination that your parents are in any danger, but that doesn't mean that I couldn't have someone watching them from a distance to be on the safe side."

That sounded good to me, and it wouldn't be an intrusion into their lives. I could deal with Kingston being a presence in my life. It meant that his security guards would protect my parents... Right?

With a heavy sigh, I turned around to face the man who drove me insane whenever he was in the same room as me. "Fine."

"I want you to say the words."

He took a step toward me, and another, until he was standing directly in front of me. His arms soon were pushing up against the counter, enclosing me. The only way I could get away from him was to either duck under his arms or shove him. But I did neither.

"I don't know what you want me to say."

"Playing dumb isn't a good look for you. I want you to say that you need my help."

I licked my lips, which had suddenly become dry. He leaned closer and I felt a shiver run down my back. "I..."

I hesitated because I didn't want to admit anything or show weakness. But I didn't have much of a choice. "I need your help."

The words rushed out of my mouth before I could stop them. It was almost like ripping a Band-Aid off, yet the weight of what I had said still sat on my chest. The relief that I thought I would've felt wasn't there. And that probably had to do with the look in his eyes.

"Good job, Princess. Admittance is a great first step. Now on to the next one."

"What's that?" I found my voice again.

"You're going to let me do what I deem is right. If I say that you need to have someone as your security wherever you go, that's what you're going to do. No questioning, no trying to get rid of your detail. Nothing. Is that clear?"

Having someone talk to me this way would normally anger me. Having it come from him should have pissed me off enough to throw a punch, but it didn't. Instead, having him take charge and stare at me the way he was made my skin warm. I didn't answer him with words this time. A slight nod of my head was the only response he got to show that I understood and agreed.

When he took a step back, I felt the air rush back into my lungs. It was as if I had stopped breathing due to the trance that he had induced on me.

"You know that none of this is going to be free, right?"

For whatever reason, I hadn't been expecting that. Had I really thought that he would do this out of the goodness of his heart?

"What do you want?"

He made a great show of giving the impression that he was thinking. His hand made its way to his chin, and he gently stroked it. His ministrations almost made me wish that he would stroke something else. Almost.

"I'll get back to you on that."

"Look, if it's money that you want —"

"I didn't say anything about money. What I did say is that I'll get back to you with the form of payment."

When he started to walk out the kitchen, I said, "This conversation isn't done. I need to know what you want."

He looked at me over his shoulder and said, "You'll find out in due time."

And with that, he left me standing in front of my container of orange juice, wondering what the hell had just happened.

7

KINGSTON

I could feel her shooting laser beams at the back of my head as I brought my suitcase across the threshold. I always kept some clothes in my car in case of emergencies and this qualified as one. It felt good having the upper hand in this situation even if she was pissed at me. Having to deal with her fire and rage before she turned into mush in my arms was worth it no matter how long it took.

Did I want my father to be after her? Of course not. But I was always one to take advantage of a situation that was handed to me, no matter the cost.

For a second, I thought back to my wife's accident and how it could have been avoided if it hadn't been for my father. Or hell, if I never married her to begin with. Now he was attempting to unleash hell on everyone else around me and Uncle Martin. It was clear that he thought he hadn't taken enough from us and that his mission in life had become to do whatever it took to take us all down. But there was no way that I would let that happen.

Most people come together in times of crisis. This wasn't

the case with Neil Cross. He and I had never had a glowing relationship, but it got worse soon after my mother's death. He never recovered after I went to live with his brother's family. The years that we didn't hear from Neil were great, although I always wondered if one day my father would come to his senses and become the loving and doting father that Uncle Martin was to me and my cousins. It never happened.

Part of me knew that I should tell Ellie the whole story. About how I now knew who was coming after her and his relationship to me. But I knew it would open a can of worms that she wasn't ready to hear nor deal with. When the time was right, she would know. Until then, she had to deal with the way things currently were.

"You don't have much stuff. Think you'll find out who's behind this pretty quickly?"

I looked up at her and found her sitting on the couch with the blanket that I used the night before across her legs. She was eating what looked to be ice cream in a bowl. I couldn't help but to think about how beautiful she looked right now. I almost felt bad for keeping shit from her, but it needed to be done. Omission was technically a lie, yet I did it anyway. "We hope to find out quickly, but I usually pack light."

"I'm not sure why you feel the need to babysit me. You could've had Nick as my bodyguard again."

The thought of Nick being on her security detail instead of me made me see red. The biggest reason why Nick was on her detail when Anais was in danger was because we suspected that she was the target versus Ellie or her family. But now I was protecting what was mine and soon would be playing for keeps even though she didn't realize it. Yet.

"We decided to have Nick watch your parents again."

Another lie easily fell from my lips. It wasn't a decision that we made. I'd given him orders and that was where he went, no questions asked. And if she made a bigger fuss about it, I would make up an excuse as to why he couldn't be here.

Why was I worried about Ellie finding out? The question bubbled in my mind as I brought my book bag to the counter and started pulling out my things. Once I had my laptop all set up, I sat down at the bar top and got to work.

"Is that all you're going to do while you're here?"

I fought the grin that wanted to appear on my lips. I'd given her plenty of space to do whatever she wanted and tried not to intrude on her private time, but something in her forced her to interact with me. It was almost like we were two magnets attracted to one another.

"I do have a business to run... Do you have something else in mind?"

I looked over my shoulder and found her with her eyes closed, shaking her head. "No. I was just...curious."

"There is nothing wrong with being curious," I said before I went back to typing on my laptop. I needed to send out a set of emails before I did anything else.

"Do you want to set some ground rules for the time that you're staying here?"

This time I answered without shifting my attention away from my computer. "Sure, but I have a few things to wrap up before I can get to that point."

"Okay."

I heard the clacking of her spoon against the bowl, and I assumed she went back to eating her ice cream. I sent off the emails I needed to send off in record time and stood up before walking over to where I left my suitcase.

"We can chat about it now."

When I turned around, Ellie was stretching, and the blanket slipped off her and onto the floor. What was exposed almost made me groan. She was wearing a sweatshirt that when she stretched didn't cover much of her torso and short shorts. Part of me wondered if she had chosen this outfit on purpose. Then again wasn't she supposed to hate me?

I forced myself to stare into her eyes and not think about her body, which was a huge struggle. "What rules do you want to discuss, Ellie?"

"I want to say that I think it's good to have rules because we will be sharing a small space for quite some time."

"That makes sense."

"I know that you don't like me as much as I don't like you and—"

"Don't put words into my mouth."

She stared at me for a few seconds. It didn't take long for her to recover, however. "Well, as much as I don't like you, I want us to be able to live peacefully while you're staying here."

I nodded again and waited for her to continue.

"First, I think you should stay in the guest room. I'll make room for you so you can at least have a bed, even if it's a bit cluttered."

"Appreciate it." I'd let her have that one. Compromise.

"Second, I still want my privacy."

"What do you think I'm going to do? Stalk your every move?"

"I don't know what gets you off." The look on her face told me that she was mentally patting herself on the back. "Third, stop looking at me like that."

I grinned at her. "I'm not sure I'm following what you're talking about."

"You know exactly what you're doing."

I folded my arms across my chest. "I'm just watching you because you're talking to me."

Ellie sighed and walked toward her kitchen.

"Listen."

She stopped moving.

"I'm willing to keep this professional if that's what you want."

"Of course that's what I want."

I scoffed. "You're such a terrible liar."

"How fucking dare—"

I was in her personal space within seconds, and I couldn't stop the jolt that surged through me when I saw her tremble slightly with me nearby. It gave me a thrill to see what kind of effect I was having on her.

"I'm going to have you begging for me to take you. Mark my words."

∼

THE NEXT DAY, I accompanied Ellie on some errands. If the glares that she was serving me were any indication, she was ready to kill me in this car and the only thing that was saving me was murder being illegal.

Ellie sighed loudly, but didn't say anything, like she'd done for the last thirty minutes.

"What is wrong? We went to all of the locations you wanted to go to today including a couple of clothing stores that weren't originally on the agenda."

She looked up from her phone and said, "You don't have to be a complete asshole about everything. You make it seem as if it was a big deal that we stopped somewhere else."

"We had a plan and we veered away from it so that is why I said something. That's all."

"Didn't seem like that was all it was, Kingston."

I usually did my best to remain neutral at all costs, but even she was starting to get to me. I counted to three before I looked down at the center console before shifting my eyes back to the road. "Do you have anywhere else you need to go?"

With a huff, she said, "No. Back to the apartment is fine."

I tapped my fingers on the steering wheel before pulling to a stop at the light. My team was at her apartment right now, doing a thorough search, and I didn't tell her about it before I authorized it. I knew if I did, she would have put up a fight that I wasn't willing to have. I knew how dangerous my father could be given his connections and his determination and I wasn't willing to risk her life. My gaze drifted toward her, but she ignored me, her full attention drawn to her phone. She continued to ignore me when we pulled into the garage at her building and on the elevator we rode to her floor.

When I opened the front door, I heard her gasp.

"What the hell is going on here?"

Her head turned toward me, her eyes wild and ablaze.

"There was no way I was taking a risk on your life after what happened and allow you to be threatened once more. I also couldn't risk anyone being blown up in case this was a serious threat."

That seemed to calm Ellie down before we were interrupted. What she didn't know was that I'd found another piece of paper this morning before we left with a strange white substance on it. I called my team in immediately to investigate, to keep her safe.

"Boss?"

I turned to face Sebastian. Ellie raised an eyebrow as I walked away with Sebastian to talk to him in private. "Update?"

"Everything is good to go. Didn't find anything." He leaned forward before he said, "We left the cameras up that were already in place based on your notes."

"Excellent. Good work."

When someone grabbed me, I turned around and found Ellie tugging on my arm. I glanced down at our connection before looking back up at her. Our eyes met before she turned her eyes away, allowing them to dance around her apartment.

"When are they leaving?"

There was something else in her voice that I couldn't pinpoint. "They should be wrapping things up shortly."

She visibly relaxed until her eyes landed back on me. "You should have told me that you were going to have people in here going through all of my things."

"This is for your protection."

She grabbed my other arm and turned me, so I was facing her. "Doesn't give you the right to not bring this up to me before you acted. My life is, once again, being turned upside down and you should have had the decency to tell me."

Her words came out in a hushed tone, as not to draw attention, but the fire was back. It was easy to read the anger behind her eyes.

"I never said I was a decent man."

She scoffed. "That's apparent."

Ellie brushed past me, and I let her go.

"Is my bedroom clear?" she asked out loud and several people that were in the living room looked up.

"Yes, miss," Sebastian confirmed.

Without another word, Ellie opened her bedroom door before closing it behind her, officially hiding herself from the rest of the world. I thought about the interaction we'd had, and I knew that I could have asked her if she was okay with having her place searched for anything that could lead us to my father. But I didn't want to give her a chance to decline the help. It would be hard for my father to get to her while she was in the building due to the heightened security we had put in place, but it helped to be safe rather than sorry.

My team wrapped up their activities and soon left. I walked over to Ellie's bedroom door and knocked.

"Yes?" Her response was sarcastic, and I hadn't expected anything less.

"Everyone is gone."

"Good."

I waited to see if she would say or do something else and when she didn't, I couldn't help but wish that she had given me more of a reaction.

Instead of continuing to wait by her door, I walked over to where I'd stationed my things. I went back to reviewing my emails before the sound of my ringtone filled the air.

When my phone rang, I glanced at the closed door that Ellie hid behind. Although it had been a couple of hours since she'd walked into her bedroom, there was still a chance that she wasn't asleep.

Before I could answer, a voice said, "I'm surprised at how easy it was to find your phone number. I thought I taught you better than that."

"Neil."

"Good to see that you still recognize your father's voice."

"Cut the bullshit, Neil." I quickly typed up a message to my team, alerting them to start running a trace on this call.

"You know there was one time when you would call me Dad."

"Those days are long gone." Neil hesitated so I continued, "Whatever you're trying to do will fail so quit while you're ahead."

"I've already won. I have you thinking about what my next move will be... How I might hurt the woman that you think you're protecting now."

"What is it that you want? What made you climb out of the hole you crawled into?"

"That's no way to talk to your father." The tone of his voice reminded me of my childhood...memories that I thought I'd done my best to bury and ignore. "But I understand that all of this is probably a shock, so I won't hold it against you."

I doubted that to be the case. "What do you want?"

"I could say revenge for everything that was done to me, but that would be dishonest. I want you to know the truth. The truth about everything."

"So you plan all of these attacks against your family in order to do so? You got everything you wanted when you promised to stay away."

"Is that what Martin told you?" Neil chuckled lightly, as if he were laughing at a shitty joke to avoid hurting the other person's feelings. "You only know half of it."

Before I could reply, he said, "I'll always be one step ahead of you. Always have, and always will. All you have to do is think of Hayley to be reminded of that."

"Listen, fucker, if you hurt anyone in this family, I'll—"

"Oh, you're specifically talking about Ellie Winters, right? But she's not quite family, is she? I saw that one of my friends paid her a couple of visits over the last few days. Did she get her purse back?"

"Neil, if you try any more funny shit—"

"Your threats are frivolous. Think about what I said. We'll speak again."

The call disconnected and I was fuming, but I was left hoping that there was enough to go on for us to get an idea of where he might be located. I tapped a couple of buttons on my phone and drummed my fingertips on the counter, waiting for the person on the other end of the line to pick up.

"Tell me we have him, Trish," I snapped when I saw that our call was connected. Trish had been a member of my team for the last couple of years and had turned into the only person who could provide me with any information I needed and quickly.

"Boss, the call location says Nebraska."

I cursed. "There is no way he's not in the tri-state area right now if I know him like I know I do. More than likely he's in this fucking city. Son of a—"

I took a deep breath and looked back at Ellie's door. A sense of calm that I usually displayed took over me and I turned my attention back to my phone. "Keep trying. I'm willing to bet he is using either a burner phone or some type of app to create a fake phone number that appears on a caller ID."

"On it."

I hung up and my fingers flew over my keyboard. I was determined to find my father before he could strike again.

8

KINGSTON

"Don't be weird about this. We're going to my job, and I need to maintain a level of professionalism."

I glanced at her out of the corner of my eye. "When have I ever been weird about something in regard to you?"

"The frequency in which I ran into you before all of this shit went down could be classified as weird."

I scoffed. "Hardly. You know I work on the security of your apartment building."

"And you just so happen to be there when I'm going to or coming home from work."

"Everything in this world isn't about you, Ellie."

She pursed her lips, probably in an attempt to control her temper. I wanted her to unleash that anger while I fucked her in this vehicle. She wasn't ready for that, though, and I couldn't wait until she was.

"It's almost as if you are intentionally trying to piss me off."

"Never that."

Her lips twitched and a warmth spread all over me. It was a strange feeling being the source of her amusement versus being the source of her anger.

"Back to the discussion about your job—I have a cover. Won't be weird to have me shadowing you when you aren't with a client."

"Also you're overdressed."

I looked down at the dark suit and button-down that I was wearing. "I thought you wanted me to be professional?"

She rolled her beautiful brown eyes, and I kept my smirk to myself, having bested her this time around.

"Mr. Cross."

Both Ellie and I turned toward the voice that was approaching us. I immediately composed a file in my mind about the woman who was approaching us. Her blonde hair was pulled into a tight bun, and she couldn't be more than average height with a slim build. I recognized her from a couple of the meetings I took when it came to purchasing this building.

"I'm sorry that I missed that you were coming today."

"I didn't tell your secretary." I looked over at Ellie and found her eyes jumping between me and the woman in front of us. "Ellie, this is Regina. Regina is one of the people helping to make the sales transition easier. Regina, this is Ellie. She works at Devotional Spa."

"Nice to meet you." The two women shook hands, and I could see Ellie sizing up Regina.

Interesting.

"Mr. Cross, do you have time for a tour of the building?"

"Why would he want that?"

I was surprised it took Ellie this long to speak up.

"It's because he bought the building, and we are in the process of finalizing the rest of the paperwork."

Ellie's eyes became as wide as saucers. I was expecting her to blurt something out, but she held it together.

"It'll be a worthwhile investment, I'm sure." I gave the woman a charming smile before I leaned over to say in Ellie's ear, "Damien mentioned that I should take a look at commercial real estate and here I am."

I could see that Ellie was ready to argue but Regina spoke first. "If there is anything that I can do for you today, please let me know."

I nodded slightly as Ellie mumbled under her breath. Her behavior was amusing.

When Regina walked away, I held out my hand, gesturing for Ellie to walk in front of me. It was easy to see how tense her body was as she walked toward Devotional Spa. Before we could enter the front doors, Ellie swung around, almost hitting me with her bag.

"I don't know what game you're playing at, but you must think I'm an idiot."

"I know for a fact that you're not, although depending on how this conversation goes..."

She let out a small scream that I was sure if she was in a private location she wouldn't have held back.

"I don't think you bought this building randomly."

"You're allowed to think whatever you want." I shifted my body to hold the front door open for her.

"You know what? I'm not going to have this conversation with you because all it is going to lead to is me getting angry and you trying to twist my words into something that they're not. I'm going to get to work, and you need to find somewhere that isn't in the way."

Before I could answer, she stormed off, leaving me holding the door and staring at her. "I don't think I've ever seen her that mad."

My eyes landed on the person who spoke, sitting behind a large white desk. Her mouth was agape, and her eyes darted between me and the door that Ellie had walked through. Behind her was a sign with the spa's name on it in large letters.

"I tend to have that reaction when it comes to her. And you are?"

"I'm Jill."

I allowed her to have the illusion that I didn't know who she was, but I had done my research. She was a bubbly, petite redhead who took her job very seriously. She'd perfected the art of being kind and warm to every person she wasn't suspicious of. I fell into the latter category.

"Are you a client? I think I would've seen you before, but there's a first time for everything."

"No, I'm the new owner of this building. I am visiting some of the businesses that are located here to get a feel of what they're doing." The lie fell off my lips easily, but it wasn't as bulletproof as I'd hoped it would be. Whether or not she would accept the explanation was a question.

"I didn't get any emails about anything like that happening today..." Her voice trailed off as her attention was drawn back to the computer in front of her.

"You can check in with Regina. She'll verify. Ellie can too." I knew she would even if she's pissed off at me right now. Ellie was very smart and if she tried to cross me as a way to get rid of me for protecting her, she would be putting her own life at risk along with her family's, and I don't take too kindly to putting unnecessary risk on her life.

"I'll confirm with both Ellie and Regina. Please have a seat over there and I'll be with you shortly."

Although it was a hassle, I liked that Jill was doing her due diligence. However, sitting down wasn't an option. Instead I walked around the waiting area of the spa, wondering what sort of security measures I could implement to help keep Ellie safe.

Jill's phone calls took a few minutes, during which time I ended up finally sitting down in one of the seats in the reception area and pulling out my phone. I sent Trish a message about my findings regarding the spa's weaknesses in their security. When I'd read up on the building, the soon-to-be-former owners had done well with the upkeep but hadn't done a whole lot in terms of beefing up security, which meant the level of security here was well below my liking. I needed to get some members of my team out here to, at the very least, put cameras up. It annoyed me that I would have to wait until the sale of the building went through to step things up.

"Mr. Cross?"

I looked up from the device.

"Everything you said checked out."

"Ellie verified my story?"

Jill nodded. "She did."

Good girl. "I'm going to take a look around and then set up shop here, if that's okay with you?"

"That's fine. I can try and see if I can get a key to our manager's office to let you have your own desk."

I weighed my options. "That might work if it's not too much of a hassle. Where is the office located?"

Jill pointed toward the door Ellie went through. "Just on the other side of that door.

That might give me a better vantage point to keep an eye on Ellie when she was in between sessions. But would it make more sense to stay near the front door so I could see who was coming and going? "Thanks, but I think I'll stay here."

It would be annoying for her to look at my mug for hours, but she'd have to deal. After all, this was about keeping Ellie safe.

"Suit yourself. Let me know if you need anything."

9

ELLIE

The silence in the car was more than welcome. At least by me. The things Anais told me about Kingston being quieter around her when he was her bodyguard were making more sense and I couldn't be happier. If he was quiet, then the chances of us snapping at each other greatly diminished and I didn't have to worry about forming a witty comeback in response to one of his.

It was day four of having Kingston come with me to work and drive me home and although he was annoying me still, I was growing more used to having him around. He mostly stayed out of my way, both in the office and at home, but his lingering presence caused a mixed bag of emotions. I still couldn't stand him but felt safer with him nearby. It was a weird predicament.

Things had been quiet on the front of whoever had tried to harm me. I had a feeling that that silence wouldn't last forever, but the thought did bring me comfort for the time being. I still looked over my shoulder a lot and was a little worried about being alone with customers while I gave massages but knowing that Kingston wasn't too far made things easier. Now, after a long day of work, I was looking forward to getting back home. Except I didn't recognize the scenery that was flying past my window.

"This isn't the way back to my apartment."

"Right you are."

We were starting with that shit again. "It's too late for your bull—"

"We're going to my place. Need to pick something up."

I was glad getting the answer out of him was easier than I expected. "So it won't take too long?"

He shook his head, and I could deal with stopping by his apartment for a pitstop. I'd been looking forward to going home, but it could wait. I was a tiny bit interested in seeing what his apartment looked like, however there was no way I was telling him that.

My eyes felt heavy as I leaned my head against the headrest. The next thing I knew, Kingston was putting his car into park.

"How long was I out?" I asked, a yawn following soon after. My body couldn't decide if that nap was helpful or made me feel even more tired.

"Maybe ten minutes, fifteen tops."

That might have been one of maybe three civil conversations we've had since he barged into my life. Once again, I was grateful that it hadn't descended into an argument because there was always a strong chance of that with him around.

The building reminded me of a slightly updated version of

my old apartment that I shared with Anais. It was well kept and at least from the outside, it looked like it was safer than my old one by a long shot. Before I could stop myself from judging, I wondered why he chose to live here instead of getting a nicer apartment. After all, if he could afford to buy the building my job was located in, he had to have had money.

I don't know what I had been expecting when I walked into Kingston's apartment, but it hadn't been this.

My eyes scanned the entryway and looked into the living area, quickly taking inventory. It was pretty easy to do since there wasn't much to look at yet, it still spoke volumes and helped me paint a picture of the man in front of me.

"Done looking around?"

I turned to face Kingston and shrugged. "To be honest, there isn't much to look at."

My response was an understatement. Kingston's apartment was nice, but there really wasn't much to look at. While he had furniture and appliances, there were no photos, of family or otherwise, art, or anything that would make this place a home, in my opinion. I understood that many people weren't into decorating or being fussy about their living space, but when someone had the means to hire out, it seemed strange to me.

"Fair."

We were back to his one-word answers. "Why is that?"

"Why is what?"

Three words were progress.

"Why don't you have many things here? Are you embracing a minimalist lifestyle? If you can afford to buy an office building, why do you choose to live here?" I paused.

"That surprisingly came out snarkier and judgy than I intended. I apologize."

It hurt to apologize to him specifically, but I had no problem admitting I was wrong here. What annoyed me was the corner of his mouth twitched. "I've found that over the last few years, I moved around frequently and didn't want something that was tying me down."

"What's wrong with being tied down?"

Kingston took his time watching me before he responded. Before his stare would have annoyed me because it felt as if he was studying me, trying to find a weakness that he could prey upon. This time, things felt different.

"Because it's something that someone could take away at any point because nothing lasts forever."

And now I knew why there had been a shift in the air in the room. The sliver of vulnerability that he had shown me wasn't something I expected, so to have him share it with me was surprising. I was glad that he trusted that tidbit with me, although it opened up a Pandora's box of questions that I didn't have the answers to. My curiosity wanted me to find out more, but I didn't want to let him know that.

"But the opposite could be the case."

"Not for me."

Goosebumps appeared on my arms, and I fought the urge to rub them. He'd effectively shut down this line of conversation. His stare had turned cold, enough to make it feel as if the temperature in his living room had dropped ten degrees. I refused to be intimidated, yet still wondered what had happened in his life that made him act this way.

"I got what I needed. We're going back to your place."

I walked over to his front door without uttering another

word and opened it. He held the door open from behind me as I walked through. Our eyes met and I refused to look away.

In his, I saw a world of hurt for half a second, something that I was willing to bet he hadn't wanted me to see. But now that I caught a glimpse of it, there was no way that it was leaving my mind.

10

ELLIE

If I ate another bite of Chinese food, I was going to pass out. I glanced over at my friend and asked, "Why do most of the things we do revolve around eating or drinking?"

Anais answered matter-of-factly, "Because that's what we love to do."

I nodded and closed my eyes, allowing the sudden tiredness I felt to win this round. It was a few days after Kingston had given me a glimpse into his world. Anais had offered to get us takeout and wine to catch up, much like we used to do when we lived together.

"How are things going with Kingston living with you?"

"Fine. He's nowhere near as good of a roommate as you."

Anais smiled as I continued.

"His company sucks."

"Are you two still bickering? Ellie, you should move past the whole scene at Elevate."

"No, keeping a grudge is better, and he gives just as good as he takes. It's sort of become our 'thing' now."

"You have a thing?"

I looked at the closed door of the guest room out of the corner of my eye. Kingston took his operation to his bedroom when we coordinated Anais's visit, giving us time to talk among ourselves. Right now, I was grateful for that.

"What do you know about Kingston?" My voice was barely above a whisper in hopes that he didn't have supersonic hearing and could interpret what I said through a closed door.

Anais looked up from her glass of wine and I could see her thinking of how to answer the question. "I guess I know a bit about him since he was my bodyguard for a while. He was mostly quiet and talked only when necessary."

He has no problem talking to me. Especially when he was talking shit.

"He was nice, but somewhat standoffish at least at first. It was definitely hard to even get him to crack a smile." Anais leaned forward and placed her wine glass on the table before she turned back to me. "You know what? I'm friendly with Grace. I could send her a text message and ask for more info on him. If you tell me why you want to know."

Her knowing smile annoyed me but I knew she could read me well. Grace would be a good person to ask since I remember hearing that she practically grew up with the Cross family due to her brother's relationship with Broderick. "He's staying with me now, so I wanted to learn about him because he's practically a stranger."

"Uh-huh." Doubt was laced in her words, but I didn't feed that beast any further. Her fingers flew across her keyboard as she typed out the message and dropped her phone on the couch. "Can I get you another glass of wine?"

"What kind of question is that?"

Anais laughed as she stood up and walked over to my kitchen counter. During the time it took for her to return with the bottle of wine we'd opened, her phone made a small chime and I looked over and saw that she had a message from Grace. The slight jump of my nerves as I wondered what she might have said made me mentally chastise myself. Did it matter what she told us about him?

Anais finished refilling our glasses before she plopped down on the couch next to me and picked up her phone. As she read through the message, she tilted her head and her eyes narrowed, making me wonder what exactly it was that she saw.

"What did she say?"

Instead of responding, Anais handed her phone to me so I could read the words for myself.

Grace: *Kingston is several years older than Damien, so I didn't interact with him as much as I have with Broderick and Gage. He's quieter than the others and I know that his wife died about six to seven years ago. I think that was when he threw all his time and energy into creating Cross Sentinel. Why?*

I handed the phone back to Anais, who typed out a reply to Grace. I couldn't focus on what she was typing because questions swirled in my mind. I was trying to wrap my head around what had just come to light. Kingston's wife was dead?

"I had no idea that he was married at one point let alone that his wife was no longer alive," Anais whispered to me.

"Is it bad that I'm curious about how she died?" I asked, but my questions went beyond that. I knew some of the things that Anais had gone through during her relationship with Damien. Yes she was happy now, but there was a lot of turmoil and pain that my friend had to deal with along the way. Not to mention the things that have been rumored about the Cross family since who knew when, was it wrong that my mind thought that her death might have been a murder...? But I could have been jumping to conclusions here.

Then again, Kingston mentioned that in his life, nothing lasted forever, and he didn't like being tied down to one place for very long...

"We must be on the same wavelength because I just asked Grace that, but in a nicer way."

Anais's phone dinged again. This time, Anais and I read the message together.

Grace: *The official story was that she died in a car accident.*

Anais: *But you don't believe that.*

Grace: *I'm not sure what to believe, but the Cross family doesn't talk about it much. I vaguely remember hearing some things, but a lot of it was kept quiet and it wasn't something I could exactly ask about. So I'm sure there are many things I don't know about the circumstances surrounding her death.*

Anais: *I understand that. Thanks for giving us some insight.*

"I could ask Damien on the sly, but then he'll wonder how I knew about it to begin with."

I jumped slightly when I heard a door open behind me. Shit. Had he heard what we were talking about?

Kingston came into view and my eyes followed him as he walked past my couch and toward the kitchen. Before he reached his destination, he nodded at the both of us, his gaze lingering on mine when our eyes met. I tensed up but hoped that he didn't notice.

"Good evening, Anais. Ellie."

I rolled my eyes and shook my head. There was something about Kingston that ended up making me revert to how I used to act as a child. And I knew he was acting this way to rile me up.

He didn't say another word as he collected a beer from the fridge and headed back to my guest room, where he was once again out of earshot. Or so I hoped.

"Do you think he heard us?" Anais voiced my fears out loud.

"I'm not sure. But it was a big coincidence that he walked out when he did."

"But you don't believe in coincidences."

"Exactly."

11

ELLIE

When I walked out of the locker room after finishing another long day at the spa, I looked around the reception area and found it empty.

"Are you looking for him?"

I glanced at Jill standing behind the front desk, putting her coat on. For some reason, I assumed that she'd already gone home, but it made sense that she would have told me so I would be the one to close things up.

"Yeah." I didn't bother trying to hide it. I tightened my grip on my handbag as I wondered what her reaction would be.

"Is there something up between you two?"

I wasn't surprised that she picked up on something due to him taking an unusual amount of interest in the spa. Too bad she didn't know it was because my life was in danger and not because of him having a middle school crush.

"I wouldn't say that."

Jill chuckled and grabbed her own purse. "I would. He can't take his eyes off of you."

"It's not what you think." *Literally. It isn't what you're thinking.*

"He stops by here every day that you're here and bounces between working in those seats over there or in our manager's office. I'm not sure what arrangement is going on there where he can freely come and go as he pleases and use Bess's office and she allows it."

"I'm not sure what all of that is about. It's above my pay grade." That was true. I didn't know what type of arrangement Kingston had worked out that allowed him to have free rein of the place. I also wasn't surprised by it either.

That made Jill chuckle and I hoped it would remove some of the heat she was throwing my way.

"Come on, I was about to close things up and then head out."

If I could have turned into a cartoon that dramatically sighed and wiped their forehead in relief, I would have.

With a small nod, I walked over to the door and held it open for Jill. She clicked the lights off and closed the door before locking it behind her. We walked outside and before either of us could say another word, I stopped moving, raising an eyebrow at the scene before me.

"Is everything okay?" Jill looked at me at what I was staring at. "Is that your friend?"

"It is. Sorry, I didn't expect to see her." I turned to look at her. "Get home safely, okay?"

Jill nodded and gave me a small wave before she walked down the street and I walked toward Anais and Damien.

"What are you doing here?"

"We're here to take you home and stay with you until Kingston gets back."

He couldn't even give me a heads-up that he wouldn't be here today? Two could play that game. Hell, couldn't Anais have texted me too?

"I already ordered takeout and wine."

Okay she's forgiven.

Damien held open the door for both of us and Anais and I scrambled into the SUV. Damien climbed into the front seat and said, "Rob, take us to the apartment."

Rob nodded and soon we were on our way to what I assumed was my place. I leaned over and whispered in Anais's ear to confirm, "He does mean my place, right? I don't know how many properties Damien owns in this city."

Anais chuckled under her breath. "He does own several properties here and around the world, but no, we are headed back to your place."

Good. I don't need any more surprises tonight. "Do you know where Kingston is? I didn't expect to have either of you pick me up this evening."

"Something came up that he needed to attend to. It was something to do Cross Sentinel, but I'm not exactly sure of the particulars."

It was a valid excuse, but I still thought he should have informed me that something was up before he left. I was annoyed about being left in the dark, especially when he could have sent a quick message. I was also disappointed because I thought that things had gotten more cordial between the two of us due to us being around each other so much. Clearly, I was wrong.

Since he had something important to deal with, I held my initial instinct to send him a text message and instead vowed to confront him when he came back to my apartment.

When we arrived at my apartment, Damien and Anais stayed for a while until another member of Cross Sentinel came to stand guard due to Kingston still not being back yet. I glanced at the time on my phone and saw that it was late. My confrontation with Kingston might have to wait until morning. I grabbed the device and headed to the bathroom, deciding to shower before bed and calm down the anger that had been building as a result of not hearing from Kingston for five hours. To make matters worse I still hadn't come to terms with why I was angry. After all, my main goal had been to spend less time with him, and yet here I was staring at my phone, willing him to call.

When I exited the shower I felt more relaxed, but there was still some anger lingering under the surface. Once I finished drying myself off, I threw a robe over my naked body and readjusted the clip I had put in my hair to prevent it from getting wet.

As I was wrapping up in the bathroom, I heard the front door of my apartment close. I couldn't stop my mind from jumping to the conclusion that it might be an intruder coming in to finish off what he started the night of my mugging.

I knew that based on where the bathroom and the front door were positioned, there was no way that whoever had just walked in could see that the bathroom light was on. As quietly as I could, I quickly reached over and turned it off right after I locked the door, surrounding myself in darkness. At least with the door locked, I would have time to come up with a plan.

There I stood in complete silence in my bathroom as I waited to see what the person's next move would be.

After what felt like minutes, but was probably only a couple seconds, I felt around my countertop and grabbed my phone. My heart was beating out of control to the point where my hand shook as I tried to lower the light on the screen and type out a message to Anais.

There was a knock on the bathroom door, and I jumped, almost dropping my phone in the process.

"Ellie?"

When I heard his voice on the other side of the door, fear left my body and was quickly replaced by anger. I pressed a button on the side of my phone, giving me enough light to flick on the light switch before unlocking the bathroom door. I twisted the knob and the bathroom door swung open with the rush, slamming into the wall behind it.

"You," I said as my mind joined my heart in a race to see which one could careen out of control first. The words I wanted to say to him fled my brain, and I was left there trying to control my rage.

He opened his mouth to say something, but I spoke first.

"Why didn't you tell me you weren't going to be here this evening?" I couldn't do anything to disguise the hurt in my voice. I was sure it was written all over my face too.

"I didn't think you'd care about me not being there. In fact, I thought you'd be overjoyed."

I threw my hands up in anger before they landed back down at my sides. The slight pain from my phone hitting my thigh made me wince. "It still would be nice to know what's going on. You know, communication and all of that."

"My whereabouts don't concern you, Princess"

"They do when it's about my safety, asshole. And stop calling me that."

"You were safe here, I made sure of it."

"Oh yeah? Because what just happened was almost identical to how Anais was kidnapped in this same damn building!"

My words must have resonated with him because he didn't utter a word. What I said was a low blow, but I didn't care. It was important to me that he knew how I felt.

"Look, Ellie, I—"

My robe fell open a smidge and I almost flashed Kingston before I snatched it closed. His eyes were glued to my body, I assumed visualizing based on the sneak peek I'd just given him.

"You're thinking about me fucking you."

I felt my eyes widen involuntarily and slowly the corners of his mouth turned up in a grin. Once again, he was enjoying getting me riled up and was saying all of this to get a reaction out of me.

"I'm thinking about how I want to throttle you right now actually, but it's a cute guess."

He took several steps toward me, forcing me to look up into his stormy gray eyes.

"Maybe it's me who is thinking about fucking you."

I gasped slightly as I watched his eyes heat up and then extinguish, almost as if a switch had been flicked.

"Now get dressed."

∼

I THREW my blanket across my legs and sighed before I shifted again. I unzipped the hoodie I'd thrown on before I left my bedroom and walked into my living room.

For some reason, I hadn't been able to turn my brain off and fall asleep. So the next best thing was to watch something on television to hopefully calm my mind down enough to shut down. I saw a sliver of light under the bathroom door when I sat down and soon the shower turned on. It was obvious what Kingston was doing.

Things hadn't shifted much in our relationship since he'd been staying here. He hadn't let on that he knew what Anais and I were digging into, thankfully. That wasn't something I wanted to have to explain to him.

Part of that was because I didn't know the answer myself. I chalked it up to Kingston being a hard person to crack. He kept his emotions heavily guarded, and I didn't know what he was thinking at any given point unless he was being snarky toward me.

"Shouldn't you be in bed?"

I rolled my eyes. "Shouldn't you be leaving me alone?"

Once again, our childish banter commenced, and I turned my head to look at him. I found myself getting an eyeful of Kingston and he wasn't leaving much to the imagination.

With a towel wrapped loosely around his waist, his body basked in the glow of a freshly taken shower. Tattoos that I hadn't known existed were displayed in their full glory. I was openly staring at the man that I found annoying.

I closed my eyes, to collect my thoughts, and when I opened them, he was smirking back at me. Of course he'd done this on purpose. The son of a—

"You must be cold."

His voice brought me out of my thoughts, and I glared at him. But his eyes weren't focused on mine. They were focused on my breasts. And it was easy to see why he was staring. My nips were forming pebbles through my shirt. It was as if they were standing at attention or begging for him to focus his attention on them.

I rushed to zip up my hoodie and my eyes settled on glaring at him. "You couldn't even pretend to be a gentleman."

"I never said I was one. So there is no need for me to pretend."

"That's hilarious given that—"

I stopped talking when he smirked and walked into my guest room, effectively ending the conversation. I stood there stunned for several seconds. Had that just happened? I wondered how I should handle it before all of my patience flew out the window.

"He's not getting away with this." I mumbled to myself when I heard his phone ring behind the closed door. I stomped over to his door, before coming to a complete stop. He'd opened the door, now fully dressed, and grabbed me by the arm.

"We need to evacuate the building." He said it as if it were the most natural thing in the world.

My heart left my body. "Wait, why?"

"A bomb threat was called in. We need to leave—now."

12

KINGSTON

It was easy to read how frightened Ellie was. She wasn't attempting to spar with me and start another battle of words. Instead she was sitting on her couch, staring out the window. I had to admit that watching the sunrise was a beautiful, relaxing opportunity, but I was sure this was a coping mechanism for her.

She had every right to be afraid. She was in the dark about the circumstances around her and didn't know where to turn to next. That's where I hoped to be the beacon of light, to guide her out of this hellhole that my father had created.

I sat down next to her, and she didn't move. One would think that she would shrink back from me given our tense relationship, but she did nothing of the sort. Her expression didn't change nor did her body's positioning, and I took a moment to just stare at the early morning light's reflection on her face.

She looked tragically beautiful. Sadness had made an attempt to mask her magnificent features and failed. She was still the most stunning woman I'd ever seen. It was then I looked at her and found tears in her eyes. "None of this is your fault."

This time she turned to me and there was no questioning the tears. The sharpness that I'd grown used to seeing in her eyes whenever I was around was gone. The feisty woman who could keep up, who had no problem speaking her mind, but she had been reduced to sulking on her couch. It reaffirmed my determination to make my father pay and to do everything in my power to make sure that Ellie remained safe.

"But it is my fault. The call was made with someone directing them to check out this floor for a bomb. We both know it wasn't a coincidence. Someone called in a bomb threat because of me."

"We should focus on the positive. No one was hurt and while it was a disruption, the most important thing is that everyone is safe right now. And I'm making a promise to you that I will find out who did this."

There was that little white lie again.

She nodded, but the expression on her face reminded me of how she looked when we evacuated the building, as the lights from the emergency personnel cars who'd come to investigate the threat flashed over her features. I'd wished to have my team do the investigating, but there was no way that we'd been able to cover as much ground as quickly as they would have been, and the call to the police had been made at the same time that I'd been informed. It also brought more attention to the situation including a story about what happened on the local morning news.

I was faced with a strange dilemma. On one hand, I

wanted to strangle my father for all the shit he'd done, but he'd helped force Ellie to be close to me.

My eyes zeroed in on her lips and I couldn't help myself. There was a chance that the change between us was because of the events that happened last night, but I didn't care. I was used to taking what I wanted, and this wasn't any different.

But it was different with her. I wasn't celibate after Hayley's death, but none of the women I'd been with had kept my attention. That was until I met her.

My thoughts never strayed too far from the woman in front of me. It was always about her and deep down, I knew that it would always be.

I captured her lips with my own.

She sank into my kiss, giving it all that she could, which wasn't very much. I thought about pulling away, thinking that she was only kissing me because she was in emotional pain, but I was too much of an asshole to do so. I'd been craving her lips since the night we met and at the time, I couldn't tell whether she wanted to throttle me or ride my dick.

Although the kiss started out slow, it didn't stay that way. The desire to have her in any way, shape, or form was too great to ignore and had taken over. I'd wanted to kiss her since the first time she'd graced my presence, the night she tried to bulldoze her way into the basement of Elevate. Sure, she was pissed when I denied her access, and mostly that was due to Damien's request not to have Anais down there. But she didn't belong down there either, unless she was coming with me.

My hand landed on her cheek, anchoring our lips to one another. Her hands ended up on my chest and I felt her gently pushing me away. I let her go because of her desire to be released, and in the back of my mind, I thought that this wouldn't last long anyway. Yet, I couldn't stay away.

I could see the debate warring in her mind about what she wanted to do, and I watched to see what choice she'd make. She leaned into me and allowed me to hug her. The feel of her in my arms was not something I'd ever forget, even if it meant keeping her in the dark for a while longer and risking losing her forever.

13

ELLIE

"This one isn't going to work either," I mumbled to myself as I tried on another dress. While it was stunning, and would be perfect for the fundraiser, it was way more than I was planning on spending. The dark green dress was strapless with a form-fitting bodice that was designed to look like a corset. The skirt of the dress billowed out from the waist into an A-line and reached my midcalf.

A knock on the door drew my attention away from the dress.

"It's time to go."

"Calm down," I whisper-yelled. Kingston had insisted on waiting for me while I tried on dresses, but he hadn't planned on me trying on so many. That was his problem, not mine.

"We were supposed to leave here fifteen minutes ago."

"Don't you think I know that?"

It was about a week after the bomb threat at my building and things had quieted down. Kingston was back to his regularly scheduled programming, which included bossing me around every chance he got. The only difference now was that we'd kissed. Neither one of us brought up the brief intimate moment we'd shared, instead choosing to ignore what had happened.

Now I was standing in a dressing room at a fancy boutique, trying on dresses for an event. I was convinced that my mother kept asking me to go to these things so that I would land a rich husband, which might then lead to me changing my profession. With a heavy sigh, I glanced around the dressing room and noticed how much I didn't seem to fit in here either. It was designed in a way that mirrored a fancy parlor versus your stereotypical dressing room. The lack of a gap between the door and the floor or any of the walls made it harder to tell exactly where Kingston was, although I felt his restlessness in droves.

I flipped my dark hair over my shoulder and put on another dress. This one didn't make it easy to zip up.

A knock on the changing room door jolted me, and I placed a hand on my chest, to both calm my heart and hold the dress up. It was one that I picked up on a whim, not one I was serious about purchasing due to the price tag.

"We need to leave. We've been here long enough, and you still have a couple of more places you want to go."

"Why? Do you have such a busy schedule? I thought your life revolved around being up my ass?"

His silence caused my heart to jump into my throat. Had I crossed the line?

"Open the door, Eleanor."

"No one calls me that so don't you fucking dare."

"First time for everything. Open the door."

His words almost came out as a growl, and I swallowed

hard. He pushed on the door slightly and my eyes widened. Was he testing how stable the door was?

"Open the door or I'm taking it off its hinges and then I'll spank your ass so that anyone who walks by can see it."

Determined not to cause a scene, I opened the door.

"You wouldn't dare." My voice was low and even with a glare fixated on my face, he remained passive.

"You love to push my buttons don't you?" He stepped into the room and closed the door behind him. He glanced over his shoulder and locked the door, effectively trapping both of us in the dressing room. The only way out was around Kingston, and there was no way he was going to let me out. "What will it take for you to realize that when I tell you to do something, you should do it?"

"Never." I didn't provide any argument because I didn't need to. I didn't need to explain myself and if he couldn't accept it, he could kiss my ass.

"Wrong answer. Turn around."

It was easy for him to crowd me in the dressing room. It wasn't the tiniest one I'd ever been in, but he took up a considerable amount of space, as well as oxygen.

"I said, turn around."

This time I did as he said. He got an eyeful of my bare back, and I could feel the heat from his gaze studying every inch of me.

"Now I want to see the front."

The front of the dress plunged a bit near the cleavage and had a big split up the leg.

Kingston said nothing, instead he allowed his actions to speak for him. He kissed me, with much more intensity than the one we shared in my apartment after the bomb scare. His kiss was almost punishing in nature, but instead of feeling pain, I felt elation. It felt as if something I'd been needing for a long time was finally within reach. However, taking the time to dissect that feeling right now was out of the question. There were more important matters to attend to.

"You're an asshole, you know that, right?"

"So you've told me multiple times. Are you complaining, Princess?"

"Not one bit." I ignored his nickname for me as I put my hands on his cheeks and shifted his lips so they landed directly on mine. He groaned in my mouth and my hands slid from his face down to his chest.

Part of me worried about ruining this dress. The other part of me couldn't give a shit as he turned me around to face him and I watched his hands disappear under the bundle of fabric.

When his hand moved up to my leg, I shivered. I should have stopped what was about to occur, but I couldn't bring myself to do so. It had been so long since I'd had any form of sex that wasn't me bringing pleasure to myself that I could burst. Adding on the danger of getting caught was at an all-time high and I could admit that I'd never had sex in a dressing room before.

When his hand landed on my thigh, his stare intensified. How could his touch almost send me into a puddle on the floor?

As if he heard my thoughts, he said, "How ready are you for me? We're going to need to make this a quickie because who knows when the sales associate will be back. Don't want to make her jealous enough that she wishes that she could join in on the fun, do you?"

"No." I shook my head and he leaned down and kissed me again. I didn't think another kiss would top how I felt when he kissed me after the bomb scare, but I was oh so wrong.

It was then that I felt his hand move from my outer thigh to my inner and his other hand joined the party. Both hands took their time reaching my center, to the point that I wanted to yell at him to hurry up. Based on the look on his face, he was enjoying the torture that his hands were giving to me.

"I thought you said that we had to get out of here soon." My own voice sounded more husky to my ears.

"I did say that, didn't I? Well then, we should speed this up."

His words were like a jolt to my system, and that was when his fingers finally went into action. I could feel one hand moving my black cotton panties out of the way before his other fingers went straight for my clit.

My head fell back, and I bit my lip to keep from crying out. When he began to play with me, my breathing became more erratic. I was slowly but surely starting not to care where the hell we were as long as this ended with me finding my release. I moaned and then moved my head so that I could look at him again and found the intensity of his stare enough to help me reach my peak, let alone what his fingers were doing to my pussy. That was until he stopped.

Before I could protest, he slowly pulled my panties down my legs, and once I stepped out of them he said, "I want you to touch yourself while I put a condom on."

I stared at him for a moment before I too moved the dress out of my way so that my fingers could touch my clit. He took a step back, but his eyes didn't leave me.

"You don't know how beautiful of a sight this is."

I moaned again and watched as he pulled out a condom from his back pocket, unzipped his pants, and rolled the condom onto his cock.

When he was once again between my legs, I took a deep breath and held it as I waited to feel him inside of me. When he wrapped one of my legs around his waist and entered me in one motion, I almost cried out. He stood still for a moment with his eyes closed before he pulled his dick almost out of me completely before his body rocked against mine once more.

When he did it again, I bit my lip so hard that I wondered if I'd drawn blood.

"I can't wait until we're fucking without condoms. I need to feel you on my cock." He continued the rhythm he'd built, and I felt my body starting to careen out of control.

"Oh my—" I gritted my teeth before I could finish my sentence to keep from screaming out.

"I'll allow you to be quieter now, but when we are fucking in private, you aren't allowed to hold back your screams. Do you understand me?"

I nodded, willing to agree to whatever he said as long as he kept doing what he was doing. The energy rolling off of him was like molten lava. Nothing was about to stop me from getting what I wanted: him.

"Miss?"

I bit back the cuss words that were ready to fly. Why had she chosen now to come back and check on me?

"Answer her," Kingston whispered in my ear before nibbling on my earlobe.

"Y-yes?" I answered.

"Is everything all right?"

"Tell her everything is fine." Kingston chose that moment to slide into me again.

"Yes. Everything is fine." The words rushed out of my mouth, and I hoped she didn't hear the hitch in my voice as he was buried in me to the hilt.

"Please let me know if you need anything else."

"Thank you!"

I smashed my lips together to keep any sounds that threatened to leave my mouth as he entered me again.

"That's right," he said as he pounded into me again. In order for me not to make a noise to alert the sales associate, I covered my mouth, muffling the sounds of my pleasure. "It probably pisses you off how much you're loving this."

"Your talking pisses me off."

He chuckled and slightly changed positions before entering me again. This time his hand joined him as one hand held me steady while the other found my clit again.

"I can't wait to taste this sweet pussy."

That was all it took.

It felt amazing to finally find my release, and when I did, my hand shook as I placed it on my stomach. I became slightly sluggish as I rode out my orgasm and soon he followed, growling as he too found his climax. He stayed inside me for a moment before taking a step back while I leaned against the wall. When I looked up, I found that he was fully dressed once again and sucking his fingers. I wished they were back on my pussy.

I turned away, closed my eyes, and took a quick breath. I needed to maintain some sense of control even after he made me unravel during the best sex I'd ever had. Another breath helped me stop my hand from shaking and I leaned against the wall before looking over my shoulder again. "There's no way I can wear this dress now."

"I'm buying this dress for you."

"Wait, what—"

"I'm buying this dress for you because I can't wait to rip it off of you, inch by inch."

There was something I couldn't resist saying as I started to regain my ability. "I thought you wanted me to beg."

"There will be time for that, Princess. Now get dressed so we can get out of here. Or do you need help with that?"

I shook my head and prayed that he would leave without another word. When he did, it felt as if I could finally breathe. I'd just had the most amazing sex of my life and it gutted me that he would be the one who I would compare every other man that fucked me to. There was no way that it could happen again.

I made sure that I looked presentable in the mirror, and for the most part I think I did a good job of pulling myself together, so it looked as if I hadn't been fucked within an inch of my life. I admit that it took me longer than it should have to get dressed, and when I finally threw the black jeans and black shirt that I'd worn into the boutique on, I opened the door and found Kingston on the other side.

"Dress?" Before I could respond, Kingston stepped into the dressing room and grabbed the garment that had made us both lose control. "Still looks good as new."

"Do you want to purchase this dress?"

Both Kingston and I turned to face the sales associate, me much quicker than him. He nodded and the woman took the dress out of his hands.

We followed the associated to the register and I said, "Listen, I don't think—"

"She'll take the dress." Kingston threw his credit card down on the counter in front of us.

His eyes dared me to argue with him, but I couldn't form the words. Instead, I chose to accept the support of his body to hold myself up, because I wasn't sure that my body could function after what had just occurred. Kingston's expression turned into a smirk, as if he could read the thoughts flying through my mind.

I hated that I no longer hated him.

14

KINGSTON

I watched as Ellie led one of her patients past the front desk of Devotional Spa. Today had been a particularly busy day where it seemed as if she wasn't going to get much of a break until later in the afternoon. I'd taken the opportunity to sit in one of the spare rooms that had a small table and chair and gave me a perfect view of who was entering and leaving the facility.

When my phone buzzed on the table next to me, I glanced down at the screen and was surprised to see the name that appeared. I answered immediately.

"You got a minute?"

I waited a beat. "I have two."

Ace Bolton chuckled on the other end of the line, and I was taken aback by it. It was so rare to hear him voice any form of happiness. That didn't take away from the fact that he was one of the best guys in this business who didn't work for me, much to my chagrin.

"You mentioned to me a couple of weeks ago that you were trying to find your father."

I nodded even though he couldn't see me. I knew how many connections Ace now had in the city, and I wanted as many people keeping an eye out for him as possible. Ace had offered to help get the bastard.

"We know where Neil has been sniffing around."

I tightened my grip on my cell phone. "I'm listening."

"He was last heard trying to get into contact with Will DePalma. Don't know if he made contact or not."

"Son of a...how solid is your information?"

"You know better than to ask me that. Anyone will talk for the right price or to save their ass. Trust me, what I shared was the truth. I could have dug further but I thought you might want to handle this yourself."

I cussed again. "Thanks, get in touch if you find anything else."

"Always."

The call ended and I found the number of the person I knew needed to go with me to meet with the mafia. Before I pressed down on my screen, I said, "When I get my hands on him, he's fucking dead."

∼

SETTING up the visit to see Will DePalma didn't take much effort, especially with Damien being the one to put in the call. After Ellie had finished work for the day and I made sure she was safely back in her apartment with a guard, Damien and I met up at Will's office to attend this meeting together. He did have us wait in the waiting area of his office for a bit, but I didn't complain since our meeting was at the last minute. From what I knew about Will, it was more than likely a power move, but I didn't give a fuck if he could give me the answers I needed.

The door to his office opened and out walked the man of the hour. "Two Crosses for the price of one. Please step foot into my office."

Both Damien and I stood up from our seats we sat in after we first arrived. I nodded at Will's secretary as we walked past her desk and into Will's office. I didn't speak until Will closed the door behind him and all three of us had sat down in our respective chairs: Will behind the brown desk, and Damien and I in the two seats that were stationed in front of the large piece of furniture.

"Has Neil Cross contacted you?"

"Right to the punch. He has tried to get in touch with me, but the last thing I want to do is get involved with anything related to your family. No offense."

Damien shrugged. "Valid reasoning."

I crossed my arms over my chest. "Who did he reach out to in order to have a chance at making his way to you and when?"

Will sized both of us up. "What's in this for me?"

I glanced at Damien, who replied, "What do you want?"

I expected Will to continue speaking to my cousin, but when his eyes drifted to me, he said, "I want you to do some investigating for me."

"What? Don't you have men who feed information to you?" I didn't come here to become a lackey of the mob.

"Of course I do, but I always love more. And you'd share a perspective that I've never had before. Helps to always keep your ear on the ground and hear from various sources. Agree to do this job for me and I'll tell you what you need to know."

"I need more details before I agree to do anything."

Will pushed back in his chair and leaned down to open up one of his desk drawers. He produced a manila envelope that he placed on the desk before sliding it over to me. I opened the folder and read its contents. I could see why he wanted Cross Sentinel to take a look at this versus him sending his own guys in.

I could feel Damien staring at me as he too wondered what decision to make. But this was a no-brainer for me. I needed to know where my father was. "Deal."

"And if I hear anything from Neil, I'll let you know."

Both Damien and I stood up at the same time and shook Will's hand. Damien let me lead the way toward Will's office door. As I turned the doorknob, Will called my name. We turned around and faced him.

"I'll have my people contact Neil's and see what I can do, but according to my sources, Neil is using a man named Lionel to make connections to the outside world."

I shared a look with Damien before nodding at Will. Before we were out of Will's office, I had my phone out typing a quick message to Trish to see if we had any ears on the ground about Lionel.

I could go and find Lionel myself right now, but I wanted all of the information that Cross Sentinel had on him before we approached. Trish would have it to me before I stepped into Ellie's apartment.

"I'd love to know why Neil would go to Will after participating in the kidnapping of Charlotte. We know that he helped fund Vincent's endeavor."

"Maybe he thought that Will chalked everything up to

Vincent being behind everything. After all, it's what we originally thought too."

"Fair. Any inclination that Will knows what we know now?"

"No, but if he does find out, you won't be the only one trying to locate Neil."

"And he'll have no problem putting a bullet through his head."

15

KINGSTON

I sat in my SUV a few days later looking up at an office building. It was after hours, and I could only imagine what I might find once I walked through the revolving doors.

Once I'd cleared security, who was dressed differently than the person I'd seen sitting at the front desk just days before, I was directed to an elevator that would take me to the floor where Will DePalma's office was located. When the elevator stopped and the doors beeped open, I didn't expect Will to be standing there waiting for me.

He didn't say anything as he led me across the floor that was practically deserted. I scanned my surroundings quickly and found Will looking at me over his shoulder.

"Did you think I'd give you a glimpse into my operations?" Will scoffed. "I don't want to give you and your family any ideas. This was an ideal location for what is about to happen tonight."

"And that is? You were awfully vague when you called me."

"I heard from Lionel."

That was what I had expected. He wouldn't have called me to his office for no reason.

"What did he tell you about Neil?"

"I'll give you one better. Neil's right-hand man is about to walk through that door within the next three minutes. You can save your questions for him."

"You lured him here with a promise to meet with you, didn't you?"

Will shrugged and that told me all I needed to know.

"Remember this the next time we call on you for a favor or to look the other way with some of our business dealings, including the case I gave you last time we met."

"Noted."

"And if anything were to happen to him while he's in here with you—"

"I'm sure you'll hang it over my head even though you've done worse."

He smirked before leaving the room. Taking it upon myself, I stood up and walked over to the large window overlooking the city's skyline. So peaceful at this very moment while a storm was brewing inside of me.

I heard a light knock on the door before it opened and closed. I waited a moment before I turned around and looked directly at the man of the hour. The widening of his eyes and his mouth hanging open was the reaction that I wanted.

"Kingston."

"Funny, it seems that you know more about me than I know about you. That's all about to change. Where's Neil?"

"Will is going to pay—"

"I'm sure he's quaking in his shoes right now. Where is Neil?"

Lionel's eyes darted to the window and back to the door he'd walked through. "He's been here and there."

"Oh, this is the way you want to play." I took a step toward him. "The best option for you is to come clean about his whereabouts. If you don't, there will be hell to pay."

When his hands shifted, a switch within me flipped. I knew that the Vitale's crime family were efficient in removing any weapons that they could find when they initially pat you down before walking into the building, but that didn't mean he hadn't snuck something in. I quickly ran through the methods that I could use to kill him before instinct took over.

I rushed to the door and his body hit it with a loud thud. I banked on him not being prepared for me to make such a move and I was right. My hand landed on the gun I brought with me. I pulled it out and placed the barrel under his chin.

"That was cute, but I've had enough of your games. Where is Neil?"

I put more pressure on the gun. I hoped that the last breath he took in would convince him that the right choice if he wanted to live was to tell me where my father was hiding. Instead, he managed to push me off of him, stunning me for half a second. When he swung his fist at me, I ducked before tackling him into the door again, rattling it against its hinges. I jabbed the gun into his chin.

He was starting to turn red, and I didn't give a fuck. "I don't know where Neil is right now!"

"He has some means of contacting you, I'm sure."

"He calls me whenever he needs me to do something, but

the number changes every time." The words came out in rough spurts, and I pushed the gun further into his chin.

"So the next time he calls you, you tell him that I want to see him. And then you alert me and make it happen. Do you understand?"

When it looked as if he might argue, I pushed harder on the gun with every ounce of strength I had.

"Do you want to test me?"

He shook his head and coughed.

"Do I make myself clear?"

He nodded and I let him go, taking a step back to give him space. He dropped to the floor, attempting to catch his breath. If Will needed to have someone come in here to clean this room, I'd make sure that he sent me the bill.

I bent down to look him dead in the eye. "I'll know if you don't do what I said. And then I'll have to come and pay you a visit. Neither one of us wants that."

I stood up to my full height and stepped over him before heading out the door. I had debated killing him but thought better of it for now. Wasting time wasn't on my agenda tonight and if he didn't deliver Neil Cross to me, I would have no problem blowing his brains out.

16

ELLIE

The mood in my apartment had shifted and I didn't like it. Not even mindless television could cure the foul mood of this space. In every place I'd lived in, I did my best to make sure that my home was a source of calm for me, but now something else was amok. And the culprit was sitting across the room from me.

Kingston was quietly talking to someone on the phone, and I found myself looking over to stare at him every so often. He'd become closed off after he returned from who knows where. Once again he didn't tell me where he was going, but this time I chose not to freak out on him because it wasn't worth my time. He was going to do what he was going to do, damn the consequences. With a sigh, I turned back to my laptop, choosing to focus on some research that I was doing.

"How long will it take you to get ready?"

"Excuse me?" I hadn't realized he'd stopped talking on the phone.

"You need to go get ready because we're going out on a date."

"Whoa, wait; what?"

"I didn't realize I needed to buy you a parrot so you could have everything repeated to you. We're going out on a date."

I rolled my eyes when he repeated what he said. I took a couple of deep breaths before I folded my arms across my chest. "Is that how you ask women to go on a date with you?"

"No, because I don't usually date."

His words made me do a double take yet based on what I knew about him it made sense. *He didn't do dates, yet wanted to ask me out?* That did make sense given what I now knew about him. The butterflies in my stomach quickly died when the doubt in my gut increased. "What's the catch?"

"Catch?"

"Yes, there has to be one if you're even entertaining going out with me somewhere willingly."

"It would be a good opportunity for us to get to know one another before the fundraiser."

And there it was. I hated that I felt dejected after his answer. "We can play twenty questions here, Kingston. I'm not going out with you."

He raised an eyebrow at me. "But you don't want that, do you? You'd prefer to be out in the world doing something that you'd consider normal, and we can get to know each other while we do so. That way no one would think it's weird that I'm following you around at the event."

"You mean like Jill asking questions about your interest in me at the spa?"

"You didn't tell me about that."

I scoffed. "I was going to tell you that evening, but you left me without warning and asked Anais and Damien to take me home from work."

"Go and get ready. I promise this outing will be better than the last date you had."

"Oh, how dare you? How would you know about the last date I had?" I remembered seeing him in my apartment after my date, but nothing I'd done gave any indication about how the date had gone.

"It doesn't take much to put it all together. The fact that when I saw you, you were returning home at a reasonable hour was a strong sign that things didn't go well. Most people would try to spend as much time with the person if there's a connection. Instead you were home and probably had enough time to watch a movie before you had to go to bed at a decent hour to be prepared for work the next day. As far as I could see, he hasn't made an attempt to reach out to you since then, nor have you tried to see him. All of that screams that the date was shit."

He had a good point, and all that was true. I had heard from Michael once or twice after the date, but when I told him I wasn't interested in pursuing anything further and he left me alone. To be honest, I had been bracing for him to send me messages calling me a bitch and a slut for not wanting to date him, but he didn't. What a wonderful surprise.

Then another thought clicked in my mind. "You seem to spend an awful lot of time watching what I do."

His eyes widened for half a second before he said, "It's my job to know things about you. It could lead to finding out whoever has it out for you because I'm sure that person is tracking you too."

I tried my best to show that his words didn't have an effect on me, but they had. I licked my lips nervously and wondered if the person he was talking about was watching me. Trying to figure out the best time to strike.

Kingston took a step toward me. And then another. And another, until he was standing right in front of me. "Ellie, I'm going to do my damnedest to make sure that nothing happens to you. And when I find the asshole who's doing this, he will pay. You have my word."

There was a small gleam in Kingston's eye, one that I dared not ask about. Because if I was being honest with myself, I was scared to find out what had caused the fire to light up in his eyes.

∽

"So can you admit now that this was better than that shitty date you last went on?"

I looked at him and laughed. "Fine. It was marginally better than the last date I went on. You didn't have to rent out the entire restaurant however."

That was a lie. It was so much better than I could have ever imagined. Kingston surprised me and rented out La Cherie, a fancy French restaurant not too far from my apartment. The classic French cuisine was amazing, and it truly spoiled me for any other date that I would ever go on. I patted my lips with my napkin and set it next to my plate.

"What's one of your dreams?"

I was taken aback at the shift in conversation. "I think if money weren't an issue, I'd buy a home near my parents and live there part of the time."

"Oh, yeah?"

I nodded. "I do miss them a lot even though both of them

drive me up a wall at times. Yes, New York City isn't far, but I also sometimes grow tired of the constant hustle of the city so it would be nice to have a place to escape to whenever I wanted."

"You wanted to get back to the city as soon as possible when everything with Anais was going on."

He remembered that? "I think not being able to return to the city made me miss it more, and I love my job even when the days are longer than planned. Plus, I was living at home with my parents which poses a whole different set of challenges."

"Understandable."

"Then add onto that they hate my job and wish I would do something else. They still don't understand that they aren't going to sway my opinion and I love doing what I do and—" I pressed my lips together to stop talking. I didn't need to keep going on and on about me. "What can you tell me about you?"

Kingston didn't say anything right away. "What do you want to know?"

His question startled me because I didn't think it would be that easy. Sure, I knew about how much he preferred order and cleanliness to the point where if I left a dish in the sink too long for his liking that he would end up washing it. I tried to be a good roommate, but eventually it would bother him, so he did it himself.

"What's your favorite childhood memory?"

"Didn't think you would go with something like that."

"I didn't either. I said the first thing that popped into my head."

Kingston nodded. "I would have to say it was a vacation

that my mom took me on. It was just me and her. We drove to Lake George and had a wonderful time with each other up there."

I could tell that he was telling the truth. The memory had brought a softness to his eyes that wasn't normally there. Deep down, it made me long for him to find that type of memory again.

Kingston cleared his throat, effectively ending the moment. "So if anyone were to ask about our relationship what should we tell them?"

"We should keep it as close to the truth as possible."

"So we met at a bar, I didn't like you and you didn't like me—"

"I never said I didn't like you, Princess."

"Stop calling me that."

"*Princess*, isn't meant to be a negative term."

"Then what is it supposed to be, then? Because the way you say it makes me think so."

"You'll find out one day."

I debated digging deeper to find out what he meant by that, but something else more pressing was on my mind. "There is one thing we haven't spoken about."

"Oh?"

I leaned forward in hopes that he'd be the only one who heard me. "Us having sex in that dressing room."

Another server who'd been walking past us gasped while other people continued on their merry way. I was sure that at least they had heard much worse.

His lips twitched. "You want to do it again?"

"I—"

"You've been thinking about us having sex again."

His words sent tingles straight to my core, and he was right, I was thinking about having sex with him again.

"Is everything to your liking?"

Our server appeared to my right and I said, "Yes, I loved everything, thank you."

When I looked over to Kingston, he was staring at me as he said, "I loved it too."

17

ELLIE

Kingston's gaze studied me, lighting a trail of fire on my skin. He looked like he belonged among these people even more than I did, yet there was something that stood out about him. I couldn't quite place it yet.

Attending fundraisers on behalf of my parents forced me to cross paths with people from all walks of life, and the evenings started to blend together due to the same people attending events such as this over and over. However, being here with Kingston felt different, and I couldn't pinpoint why. People were looking at us as we walked by, probably because of how close Kingston was to me. When he placed his hand on the small of my back, I jumped slightly.

He leaned over and whispered in my ear, "Calm down, Princess. Don't want people thinking that you don't want to be here with me, do you?"

I growled under my breath and felt Kingston gently tap my lower back with one of his fingers, warning me that he'd heard the sound I'd tried to conceal.

"Ellie Winters."

I turned around when I heard my name. Standing behind us was Bella Andrews. She and her husband had known my parents for decades.

"You look stunning," she said as she gave me a kiss on each cheek. "And who is this?"

"This is Kingston Cross, my... date for the night." I felt my heart skip a beat after I said it out loud.

"Kingston Cross," she said, allowing his name to roll around on her tongue. "You wouldn't happen to be related to Martin Cross, would you?"

"He's my uncle."

"Yes, then I know your family quite well. He and I attended college together."

"At Brentson? I went there too."

"Excellent. Well, I need to say hello to more people, but it was nice meeting you, Kingston, and seeing you again, Ellie. Please tell your parents hello."

"Will do," I said with a smile.

When she walked away, Kingston said, "That wasn't so bad."

"That's true. Plus, it's an excuse to wear this stunning dress."

Kingston leaned over and said, "And I can't wait to see it in a pile on the floor just before I feast on your breasts."

I looked around to see if anyone had heard what he'd said. "Can you stop talking like that out loud? Saying those things while we're at my place is one thing, but I know quite a few of these people here, and at the very least, they know my parents, so stop it."

"You liked it and that's all that matters to me."

He was right about that. I enjoyed whenever he snuck in dirty talk when we weren't in the bedroom. It made me anticipate what he might have up his sleeve.

"There you two are."

We swung around and found Anais and Damien standing there. Anais leaned over and hugged me, and Damien and Kingston shook hands, keeping things somewhat professional since we were in public.

Damien gave me a slight smile before he looked at Kingston and said, "Can I talk to you for a second?"

Kingston nodded and whispered to me, "I'll be right back." His breath tickled my ear and sent a slight shiver through my body. He patted me on my lower back before he walked away, and I found Anais staring at me suspiciously.

"Why didn't you tell me that you and Kingston had sex?"

I almost choked on my champagne. "What? I didn't say anything."

"Your response just did."

I closed my eyes and took a deep breath. I tried to calm myself to hopefully prevent the headache I could feel coming on. I'd let my guard down, and Anais had used one of my tactics to find out information against me.

"I knew something was going on between the two of you. That moment when we were standing in the mansion as you were helping me move in? Sparks were flying."

"I would prefer not to think about that because soon after that you ended up in Damien's office playing Russian roulette with Vincent."

"I know. Well, we don't have to think about that aspect, but we can talk about your budding relationship with Kingston."

"There's nothing going on between me and Kingston."

Anais snorted. "Okay, sure. It's not like he's staring at you right now, for instance."

I turned to verify what she had said, and sure enough Kingston was looking at me from where he was standing with Damien. "You do realize he is supposed to be my bodyguard, right?"

"He was my bodyguard at one point too and he wasn't looking at me like that."

"If he was looking at you, Damien would've had a field day with him."

"That's a good point. But it doesn't take away from what I am observing between the two of you. And you never denied that you two had sex."

I sighed, rather dramatically if I had to admit it to myself. "Fine, we did. It was glorious, okay? And I can't wait to do it again."

"Ha! I knew it. Oh, how the tables have turned, sweet best friend of mine."

I rolled my eyes, but it didn't make sense to lie to Anais. After all, it was only a matter of time before she found out anyway.

"These Cross men have a way of seducing women when we are in danger."

I glanced at her before taking another sip of my drink. "Isn't that part of the thrill though? Yes, you love Damien now, but being brought together in such a tumultuous way can be exhilarating."

"I could see that. Is that what it's like for you and Kingston?"

"Wow. I'm not sure what is going on between Kingston

and me. Nothing has been defined, but all I know is that we've had fantastic sex with one another. I could do without the danger aspect that threw us together, but the sex is... something else."

"It sounds to me as if there is more going on there than just awesome sex."

I glared at Anais.

"Yeah, because I said the same thing myself with Damien."

"Anais, can I get you a drink?" Damien appeared at her side and that was when I felt a hand slide across my lower back. I didn't need to look to know that it was Kingston's hand. It was as if he'd marked me, and I could identify him with my eyes closed. *Shit.*

"Do you need a refill?"

The low timbre of his voice brought back memories of the fun we'd had in the dressing room and his dirty talk moments before. Would it be too crass to find an abandoned room in here and have a quickie? It would calm my nerves and make this event more bearable.

Of course that was when someone walked up to the microphone on the stage at the front of the room and tapped on it. "Welcome, everyone! The program is about to begin."

I bit back a growl at having my dreams of a quickie being crushed. That was until Kingston leaned over once again.

"Let's get you that refill and we can talk about what has that dazed look in your eyes later."

∼

LATER NEVER CAME, but I knew that I was going to.

Once we'd entered my apartment, all sense of decorum went out the window. I somewhat wished that we could have found some place at the fundraiser to release this energy that was building between us. And I knew he could feel it too.

When the front door slammed shut, his hands were all over me on a scavenger hunt to get me naked and underneath him as fast as possible.

"This fucking dress is going to be the death of me. Every time I see you in it, it makes me want to rip it off."

Before I could think of a response, he kissed me, removing any words or thoughts that I possessed. Not that I was about to complain about it.

He backed me into a wall and when he stopped kissing me, he unzipped the dress part way and pushed the bodice down, leaving me with a strapless bra on. Within no time, the bra was lying at our feet and my nipple was in his mouth.

"Kingston..." My voice trailed off when his tongue flicked across my nipple again.

"Say the words, Ellie."

I shook my head, refusing to give him what he wanted.

"If you don't say the words, I'll stop. Right here, right now. I don't give a damn."

"Kingston, I want you to fuck me."

"Finally."

Kingston's lips slammed into mine again, telling me exactly what he thought of my response. His hand settled on my throat while he was kissing me before it slowly made its way to my breasts. He massaged my tit before tapping it and I gasped at sensation. Then he played with my nipples before moving down so he could put it into his mouth.

He used his other hand to play with my other breast, so it

was only a moment before I watched as my nipple became a stiff peak. Once he switched gears to the other breast, he looked up at me and I could feel him reading my expressions, probably wondering how much he was driving me wild.

My nipple fell out of his mouth with a *pop,* and he lowered himself until he kneeled before me.

"I can't wait to taste you, Princess." He buried his head under my dress, and I could feel his breath tickling my inner thighs. He wasn't wasting any time and I was thankful.

His fingertips touched my panty-covered mound, gently rubbing his finger up and down my slit. When I felt his tongue lick me through my panties, I thought I might be able to climax right then and there.

I felt him pull my panties down my legs, reminding me of a groom retrieving the garter from his new bride. When he surfaced from underneath my dress, he asked, "Did you wear this lacy thing for me?"

I was so turned on by seeing him holding my soaked panties on his index finger.

"Maybe."

"I enjoyed the present, but there is something I want more. Turn around."

I didn't hesitate to do as he commanded.

"Walk over to the balcony door and lay your hands on the glass."

I heard him unzip his pants before he said, "I don't want to use a condom tonight."

I looked over my shoulder at him and said, "You don't have to. I have an IUD and I'm clean."

"So am I."

I took my time looking at his magnificent body as he

walked toward me. I lowered my eyes to his cock, anticipating just how good it would feel once he was inside of me without the barrier between us. I turned my head to look back at my hand placement and felt the body heat coming from him. He pushed up my dress, ran his dick along my butt, drawing an erotic picture that only he could see.

"Are you ready?"

His voice was low, and my anticipation had hit its peak. "Yes."

He pushed me up against the glass at the same time that his cock entered me, and the dual sensation made me scream in pleasure.

"Yes. I love to hear the noises you make. Let your neighbors know how well you're about to get fucked."

He gave me a second to adjust to his size and pounded into me again. The coldness from the glass and the heat of his body was magical, the perfect duality as he sped up his pace.

I moaned as he pushed my body to a place that it felt like it had never been before.

He had me up against the sliding glass door and I could see parts of New York City's skyline. While the city was beautiful, especially at night, my attention was drawn back to the man who was currently taking me to another galaxy with his body. My nipples got used to the temperature of the glass and I couldn't help but think that if someone had binoculars or a telescope pointed at my balcony right now, they were in for a treat.

I closed my eyes and said, "I'm going to—"

"Me too," he said before he rolled his hips and pumped into me again and we both went over the ledge together.

My heart was racing, and I wasn't sure if it would ever

slow down, especially with him in the room. He hugged me from behind before slowly removing himself from me. At least one of us could move, because I wasn't sure if I could control my limbs.

"At some point we need to make it to the bed."

I heard his words, but they came through as if he'd said them from somewhere far away. My mind was in a daze, and it took me a second to think of a response. "There's always time for that during round three."

18

KINGSTON

Ellie wasn't a morning person these days, but the way that her head fell back while I was licking her pussy probably could make her into one. I gazed at her body as the sun began to make itself known, lighting up her body with a warm glow.

She groaned as her fingers laced through my hair, showing me how much she liked how I was using my tongue. Her moans grew louder and the pressure on my head increased, telling me that she was getting close. I could hear her heavy breathing and it served as motivation to make sure that I could taste all of her juices on my tongue.

When she screamed out, I smirked against her pussy, hungrily lapping everything, so I knew I didn't miss a drop.

She looked down at me with eyes that were almost shut. "I thought I was dreaming."

"Good morning," I said, before making my way up her body and kissing her. She opened her mouth, allowing my tongue access. "Well, you taste like a dream, so I had to share.

That was a thank-you for wearing those panties last night. You don't know how good your ass looked in them."

Ellie looked at me and moved my arm so that it was lying around her. I pulled her in close, enjoying the feeling of having someone in my arms for the first time in a while. When her stomach growled, we both chuckled.

"I'll start making breakfast." I slid my arm out from underneath her, immediately missing the connection we shared.

"You will?" she asked as she watched me stand up and put a pair of boxers and black sweatpants on.

"Yes, I'm thinking omelets, if that's fine with you?" All she did was nod. "I'll get started and you should join me in the kitchen when you're ready."

"Deal."

∼

"Why are you so detached from…life?"

I shifted slightly and folded the omelet. "I'm not detached from life."

"Maybe that was the wrong thing to say. I'm sorry."

"You know a couple of weeks ago we wouldn't have been in this position."

She took a sip from the glass in her hand and nodded. "It's funny how things change, huh?"

"That's what life is all about. Change." I meant that as I felt her presence surrounding me. "Back to your question about me being detached, I can see where you got that idea, but I feel as if that's changing."

I moved to put the omelet on the plate I'd set up next to

the stove. I heard Ellie gasp when the omelet landed, and I spared a quick glance at her to see the look on her face. Seeing her light up with happiness did something to me and reminded me of what it was like to not have to worry about all of the treacherous shit that happens in this world. It felt wonderful, even if it was for a moment, to forget all of the bullshit temporarily.

"I've lost a lot over the years, and I think it has made me more closed off, in fear of losing something or someone else that I care about."

I stared into her eyes, and our connection didn't break until she looked down at the food in front of her. While she played with her food, I could see the hesitation in her movements but instead of trying to fill the silence with my own words I decided to wait until she spoke what was on her mind.

Her eyes slowly made their way back up to mine. "What happened to you that made you feel as if everything would be taken from you?"

This question wasn't surprising given the way the conversation was heading yet the answer wasn't sitting on the tip of my tongue. That was because the answer was very complicated. Most of the people I surrounded myself with either knew my backstory or at least had an insight into it or were too afraid to ask. It's why I never had to explain why I lived the way I lived. But this was different, and it felt as if she had a right to know. She also had a right to know who was after her, but I couldn't tell her yet. Not when things had finally gotten to the place I hoped they would get to for so long.

"Why don't you start eating while I whip up this other omelet? It shouldn't take long."

Ellie smiled again, not mentioning that I had changed the subject. "No, I want us to eat these together. I'll set the table and start bringing our drinks out so all you have to do is bring your food. I'll place my omelet in the microwave so that it can keep warm until we're ready."

"That's a plan," I said and turned my attention back to the stove. I could hear her moving and shuffling things behind me, I assume carrying out the tasks she set for herself. Once I was done, I joined her at the dining room table and swapped out the freshly made omelet for the one I made a few moments prior.

"I'll take the older omelet."

Ellie held her hands up. "I'm not going to argue about that."

"That's a first."

She laughed out loud, and the sound warmed my soul. What had felt so bleak and dreary for so long was starting to shift, and it was a change that I'd wanted for years.

"Can we go back to talking about you? I feel like we only touched the surface, and you seem to be almost a complete mystery to me. Yet I feel like you've been forced to know more about me based on the dangerous situations that Anais was in and now having to stay with me because someone wants to hurt me."

I wanted to blurt out everything I knew about how dangerous things were for her right now, but I refrained. I preferred to have a better handle on where my father was before telling her everything that I knew about why this was occurring. For some strange reason, I didn't have a problem with sharing parts of myself with her.

"I would say that I've experienced a lot of loss in my life." I folded my hands together suddenly, not having the urge to finish my meal. "I lost my mother when I was sixteen years old."

"Oh my gosh, Kingston. I'm so sorry. If you don't want to talk about this..."

"No, it's fine. There will always be a part of me that is grieving her death, whether I show it or not. But I have no problem talking about it. The circumstances around her death are somewhat of a mystery."

"What do you mean?" she asked. "Wait, no, I don't want you to go into detail about this. What a horrible thing for me to ask."

I reached over and placed my hand over hers. "Ellie, it's fine. To make a long story short, my mother died after falling off a building. I say that because a lot of people assumed that she committed suicide, but I always second-guessed it. Maybe this was me being naive, but I've always had this feeling that she wasn't alone the night she fell. No evidence either way."

You could hear a pin drop between the two of us after I stopped talking. I gave Ellie's hand a squeeze to let her know that talking about this was okay with me.

She brushed a hand across her neck and said, "I know this sounds silly, but I never expected you to say that, and if I can be upfront with you about the fact I expected you to talk about your wife."

Confusion must have been in my eyes because I hadn't mentioned Hayley to her, but it was clear she had done some digging of her own. It was interesting because finding out more information on Ellie had been my part-time job over the last few months, so I shouldn't be surprised that she'd done the same. "Why am I not shocked that you know about Hayley?"

"Because I'm used to being in the know about a lot of things and when you came to protect me, I knew practically nothing about you. So I had to do my research."

"Fair enough. Hayley died in a car accident years ago." I leaned back in my chair, giving me what felt like space to think. "Her car was hit by a tractor trailer and the coroner said he believed that she died on impact. The fact that she didn't suffer for long is what helped me sleep at night for years. I always wondered if that was an accident as well, but it seemed more clear-cut for lack of a better word."

I didn't tell her about how I knew it was my father that ordered the hit on Hayley. That box didn't need to be opened either and by the expression on Ellie's face, that was the right call.

Tears streamed down Ellie's face as she shifted to place my hand into both of hers. "Kingston I don't know what to say. Once again I'm so sorry."

I squeezed her hand. "There isn't much to say. Both of these incidents happened a long time ago and helped feed my motivation to start Cross Sentinel. Yes, I would trade everything to be able to talk to them once more. When everything happened with my mom, Aunt Selena and Uncle Martin opened their doors. I don't think there was any way I would have gotten past these events without them."

"You're blessed to have both of them in your life."

"I know, and I don't take either one of them for granted."

"That makes sense. Where was your father in all of this? I know that he and Martin are brothers. I found that out when

I was helping Anais gather information on Damien. Sorry not sorry."

A dry chuckle fell from my lips before I could stop it. "Neil Cross pretty much fell off the face of the planet when my mother passed away. Just another reason why I'm so glad to have Uncle Martin and Aunt Selena."

"He was devastated by your mother's death, I assume. Not that that's an excuse."

I shrugged. "I guess you could say that."

"Sounds complicated."

"That's why I mentioned it was earlier."

This time, it was her turn to laugh, and I was hoping to have the topic shift from my father to something else. The less time I spent talking about him, the better it was for both of us.

∽

I WAS IN TOO DEEP, and it was only a matter of time before things would come to an end. Or so I told myself.

Ellie and I had spent most of the day being lazy in her apartment. Things were quiet at Cross Sentinel, so I focused on Ellie and doing small projects for her around the apartment. While it hadn't been eventful, per se, I would say we both enjoyed spending the time together away from the outside world. I wasn't asleep when my phone rang, but Ellie happened to be, so she groaned when it vibrated on her end table. I reached over and grabbed it, hoping not to disturb her any further.

Unknown Number: *I've scheduled for Neil to meet you in two days. Come alone.*

Instead of replying, I put my phone on silent and placed it back on the table. I didn't know what to expect when I finally got word that I would be seeing my father but feeling disappointed hadn't been a part of the equation. It meant that all this was coming to an end and soon. No one I cared about would have to wonder when he was going to strike next. But it also meant that my time with Ellie was coming to an end.

Change.

Once again that word appeared in my mind, like a force of nature. It was always hiding behind every corner ready to fuck things up for me, but that was a battle I was prepared to face. Much like the one that would come about when I was face-to-face with my father again.

19

ELLIE

"Where are you taking me, Kingston? And why is there a need for a blindfold?"

"Because I needed to find a way to keep you on your toes. Plus seeing you blindfolded and not having the ability to control this situation, is such a turn-on for me."

I could feel the heat rising through my body, and I wasn't sure if it was a result of me blushing or me too being turned on by turning the reins over to him, so to speak. Excitement rushed through me at the thought of what he might have planned for tonight.

The car came to a stop and the butterflies in my stomach increased. Where the hell were we?

I heard a car door open and shut, and then I heard the door next to me open. I felt Kingston grab my hand.

"You're going to step out of the car, but I have you. Trust me."

I licked my lips slightly, hoping I didn't smudge my lip gloss.

"When are you going to tell me where we are?"

"In a second."

I could hear the humming of some music in the background. I could hear the bass, but it wasn't loud enough to give me a hint as to where we were.

"Remove the blindfold."

"Where are we?"

"Hold on a second."

Kingston opened a door.

"You wanted to get into the basement of Elevate. Now here's your opportunity."

I could hear my heart thumping in my ears after his words. Here we were, standing at the very door where we met for the first time, and I couldn't help but think about how much things had drastically changed since that moment. I found myself looking forward to seeing him when I woke up in the morning and lying in his arms when we went to bed at night. And now here I was, about to have the time of my life at the sex club his cousins owned.

I was almost positive we hadn't walked in through the front door. "Don't I need a coin in order to be able to get in?"

Kingston smiled, remembering our argument about that when we first met. "You need a key to get in now, which I have in my pocket for you."

He led me farther into the sex club until we reached a door that was to my left. When he opened the door, I gasped.

The room we entered was beach themed. It had everything from beach chairs to a hammock, to the sounds of soft waves in the distance. I also spotted a hot tub in the room.

"Kingston, I didn't bring a swimsuit, if you didn't notice."

"That's because you don't need one. Same rules apply as

they did at your apartment. No holding back, I want to hear exactly how you feel. Every. Damn. Syllable."

I looked down at the black dress I was wearing before looking back at him. He looked so handsome in the soft light of this beach-themed room. With a small smile, I nodded, ready to go on this journey that I was sure he would take me on tonight.

"I've always wanted to skinny-dip in a hot tub."

"Well, don't let me stop you."

He gestured to the tub that was already turned on and ready to go. An idea popped into my mind as I gave Kingston a coy grin. I spun around on my heel and looked over my shoulder at him.

"Do you think you can help me unzip this?"

Kingston walked over to me, and his hands slid up and down my back. "You didn't have much of an issue putting it on?"

"But since you're eager to please tonight, I figured I would hand over the reins to you."

That seemed to do the trick and all I could hear was the sound of my dress being unzipped and the waves that made me long to go to a beach in the middle of nowhere. My dress fell into a puddle at my feet, and I turned around to face him. All that was left was the black lingerie, another set that I thought he might love on the chance that we would have sex tonight. Little did I know that he was taking me to Elevate.

He ran his thumb across my lips. If I hadn't smudged my lip gloss when I licked my lips in the car, it was definitely smudged now, and I couldn't care less.

"You look so beautiful. I haven't said it enough and I apologize."

I took a step back, and another and another, until I turned around and walked over to the hot tub. As I walked over, I tossed my hair up into a quick ponytail. Then, I peeled off the bra and then the panties and then stepped into the tub, all the while not turning to watch what he was doing. But I would have known he was there no matter what because I felt the fire from his gaze staring into the depths of my soul with every movement I made.

When I took a seat in the tub, I turned to face him. He too had made his way over to the hot tub and was already shirtless by the time he reached it. It took him no time to unzip his pants and slip into the tub.

"I want you on my lap now."

A jolt of electricity flew through my body as I climbed onto his lap. He leaned forward to kiss me on the lips, and I sighed into it. When his kisses migrated from my lips, down to my jaw, and then to my neck, I groaned, enjoying each and every touch that he laid on me. When his hands landed on my waist, he squeezed me there before shifting me so that my pussy came into direct contact with his cock. This time, instead of me groaning, he joined me in a moan that made me smile to myself about having gotten that reaction out of him. My eyes squeezed shut when I felt him nibble on my neck before leaving a trail of small kisses down to my breasts.

With my breasts in his face, Kingston took the opportunity to suck on my nipples. His hand reached out of the water and caressed the other nipple and when he pinched it, I gasped in shock.

"Fuck, yes. Do that again."

Kingston chuckled against my skin before he sucked on my nipple again, harder this time and I was convinced that my body was ready to climax right then and there. I found myself trying to get closer to him, and I halted his movements to whisper in his ear because I was ready to get this show on the road. "I want your cock right now."

"Just the words I wanted to hear."

I rose slightly and then eased down on his cock. He moaned again, voicing his pleasure. I rolled my hips back and forth, fully enjoying what it felt like to have his cock inside of me while I sat on his lap.

"You're so responsive to my touch. Take control of me, Princess." He lightly slapped my ass before grabbing it underwater and I began riding him.

He helped guide me down onto his cock, giving me the ability to ride him harder and faster. The water in the hot tub was warm, but my body was burning up as he started to pump his hips to the same rhythm that I had set. He lightly slapped my ass again and I groaned out his name.

His hands were back on my breasts, fondling them like they were the most precious things in the world to him. His mouth was back on my nipples, alternating between each one and switching between sucking and licking them. The pressure that had been building inside me ever since he'd placed the blindfold over my eyes had reached its peak.

I yelled as I went over the edge, and the last thing I saw before my eyes squeezed shut was Kingston's knowing smirk. He knew what he had done to me without me having to say a word. I kept riding him until he reached his completion as well.

After we had cleaned up and dried off from our hot tub escapade, I found myself lying mostly on top of Kingston in the hammock, both of us content to lie with one another for the time being. As we swung back and forth, and the sounds of crashing waves played all around us. It wasn't an official vacation, but it was time away from the real world even for a short while.

After a few moments in the hammock, we got up and pulled ourselves together. The expression on Kingston's face was unreadable but changed to confusion when his phone vibrated.

"I thought I turned that thing on silent," he mumbled and read the message that he received. "Do you want to grab a drink with Gage and his girlfriend Melissa?"

A lazy smile appeared on my lips. He wanted to hang out with me in public? "You want to grab drinks with me?"

"After what we've just done, you have to ask that?"

Before I had an opportunity to respond, Kingston walked up to me and laid a kiss on my lips. It was possessive in nature removing any doubt from my mind, claiming me in a way I never expected. Any doubts about how I thought he felt about me fled my mind. The smile that he gave me after he kissed me was so wide, crinkles appeared in the corners of his eyes.

"Let's head upstairs."

"Wait, I need to check my makeup."

"Okay but make it quick. The longer you take, means the longer I need to deal with my cousin and the longer it'll take for me to get you underneath me. And when you are, I want your hair down."

I chuckled as I looked at myself in the compact mirror that I'd brought with me. I didn't look like I'd just had sex outside of my hair being slightly wet near where some of my hair's strands had come loose. When I reached up and pulled my hair loose from its restraints, I looked over at him and found him reaching over to pull my hair lightly to lift my face so that he could kiss me again.

"You don't know how much I love your hair."

"I think I do now," I said. I tossed some lip gloss on my lips and then Kingston led me out of the room where we'd spent most of our evening.

It was hard to describe how I felt as we walked up the stairs and out of the basement, to the main floor of Elevate and then up to the VIP section where I first spotted Gage. Based on her positioning on his lap, it was easy to find who I assumed was Melissa. The two were whispering into each other's ears while she sat on his lap.

"The sex club is that way," Kingston said as he pulled me in closer to his body. My own body hummed with excitement about being this close to him.

"If you call this sex, then we need to have a talk about the birds and the bees." Gage turned to me and said, "Come on and join us. I want to get to know the woman who has taken over Kingston's thoughts. We can find a booth to sit in and grab some drinks."

I glanced at Kingston out of the corner of my eye, but he didn't react. I didn't know if I wished he had or hadn't. Instead, I stuck my hand out and looked at the woman who'd just stood up. "Hi, I'm Ellie."

She smiled at me warmly. "I'm Melissa."

"I don't believe we've met before, but I apologize if we have, and I've forgotten."

"We probably haven't. I've recently started coming around to Cross family functions."

"She didn't want to be seen with me," Gage joked.

I laughed at Gage and turned my attention to Kingston, who'd been quiet for some time. I found him looking back at me and I didn't know what to make of it. After everything that had happened in the time that he'd moved in with me, I couldn't shake the feeling that something had changed between us tonight, but I wasn't sure what.

20

ELLIE

Emotions took over me once more as I wrapped my arms around myself. Kingston told me that there might have been a break in the case and that he was going to investigate. I understood that it was something he needed to do alone, but that didn't mean that I wasn't worried about him.

I thought back to the moments that we spent at Elevate together, and how that felt like it had happened so long ago even if it was only a day ago. It seemed that the sweet time we spent together there had exited his mind today and he was tense about wherever he had to go this evening. Then again, I couldn't blame him, especially if he did have a break in the case.

As I paced between my living room and my kitchen I couldn't stop my mind from going to a dark place. What would happen if Kingston didn't come home? Would I be able to go back to the way things were before? No. There was no way I could go back. My life had changed, whether I liked it or not. This was my new reality, but I couldn't let the negative thoughts take over. Everything would be fine, and I would see him soon, I thought after I did another lap from my kitchen to the living room.

I could try to read a book to take my mind off of him being gone or watch a television show. But who was I kidding? There was absolutely no way that I was going to get around not wondering how Kingston was doing until I could see him with my own two eyes.

When I was about to walk past my kitchen again, I leaned over and grabbed my phone. A small part of me hoped that Kingston had sent a message letting me know that he was all right and would be back home shortly, but he hadn't.

I'd referred to my home as being his. *Shit.*

I found Anais's and my text message thread and thought it was best to reach out to her. I assumed Damien didn't know about the mission that Kingston was on or else and she probably would have been with me right now.

Me: *Hey, Anais. Are you awake?*

When I saw that she was typing back to me I almost jumped with glee.

Anais: *Yes, I am. What's up?*

Me: *I don't know if Kingston told Damien this, but he thinks he might be closer to finding whoever is trying to hurt me, and he's currently investigating. He thinks he might have found a break in the case.*

It took Anais a few minutes to text me back.

Anais: *Damien didn't know anything about it. But he's going to try to call Kingston now. Says he wishes Kingston would have reached out.*

Me: *Would you be willing to come by and stay with me? I*

think I'd feel better having someone else here and not just a bodyguard standing outside my door.

Anais: *Of course. Let me check with Damien and either we both will come over, or I'll see if Rob can drive me door to door.*

Me: *From what I know about Damien, he's not gonna let you out of his sight, especially with Kingston away and someone coming after me.*

Anais: *True.*

Me: *Thanks.* A sense of relief washed over me at the thought of Anais being on her way. That feeling vanished when I jumped as my phone vibrated again. I checked it and found a message from my mother.

Mom: *Hi sweetie. Just wanted to check in and see how you were doing. Hadn't heard from you in a couple of days.*

I took several deep breaths to calm my already jumpy heart before I responded.

Me: *Mom, everything's* fine, pretty *busy at the moment, but I'll call you when I get an opportunity tomorrow.*

Mom: *Okay, sounds good.*

There was no way I was going to be able to have a conversation with my mom. With everything else going on right now, I was too worried about Kingston. Any stress that might arise from a conversation with my parents might send me over the edge. I loved them dearly, but I could almost guarantee that something about my chosen profession would be brought up and I mentally couldn't handle it. If it was anything else, like something about the fundraiser, I would be happy to talk about it.

My phone's screen lit up and I saw I had another message from Anais.

Anais: *Damien and I will be by shortly.*

A breath that I didn't know I was holding rushed out of me because I wouldn't have to be alone anymore. That was the only comforting feeling I felt I could feel until I knew that Kingston was all right.

In the time it took Anais and Damien to arrive, I'd found a movie to watch that I hoped would take my mind off of the circumstances at hand. It didn't but at least it allowed for me to have some noise in the background while I waited for my best friend to arrive. When I heard a knock on my front door, my heart jumped even though I was expecting company. The guard that was stationed at my door, opened it and in walked Anais and Damien.

She spoke first. "Oh, I'm sorry it took so long. We got caught in some traffic on the way over."

"No worries," I replied. "I'm thankful to have you both here. Have either of you heard from him?"

Both shook their heads and Anais took her time looking me over before she said, "We should have a glass of wine."

Did I really look that bad? I thought about her suggestion and slowly nodded my head. I didn't want to drink too much, but if having some wine could take the edge off what I was feeling right now, I didn't have a problem with that. Having gotten my confirmation, Anais walked into my kitchen and then turned to her fiancé and asked, "Do you want any?"

"No thanks, Spitfire," he replied.

A light blush appeared on Anais's face, and I smirked. Even though I was stressed beyond belief right now, it was lovely to watch the interactions that my best friend had with the love of her life. In fact, it inspired my next suggestion, which I knew would somewhat annoy her.

"You know what would take my mind off of this?" I asked.

Anais looked over her shoulder at me briefly while she was pouring the wine into glasses. "What?"

"Talking about your wedding," I said teasingly. Wedding planning had been a bit contentious with Anais not knowing exactly what she wanted yet.

She sighed and said, "That is probably the last thing we should be talking about right now."

"I told her we can hire a wedding planner to help with all of this, but you've been adamant about not doing so… at least, not yet," Damien chimed in.

"I know, I know," Anais said as she picked up the two glasses of wine and walked to the living room. She handed one to me before taking a sip out of the other.

"We're going to need to talk about it sometime," I said.

"I know that too."

I glanced at Damien before I said, "Plus, all Damien wants, I'm sure, is to make sure that you both sign on the dotted line. He could probably care less about how it's done as long as you're happy."

"She's right."

I smiled at the man in question before taking a sip of my wine. The liquid felt lovely going down my throat and it was the first time that evening that my focus hadn't been on whether the man who vowed to protect me would return home alive.

We all jumped when a phone rang, and Damien was the one who ended up removing his phone from his pocket and reading the message. He looked at Anais before he stared at me. My stomach settled into my chest as I wondered what he was about to share with us.

"It's a text message from Kingston's phone."

21

KINGSTON

As I drove toward the location that Lionel specified, my thoughts were centered around how this could finally be the end. Ellie would finally be safe if my father was off the streets. In my time, I've dealt with some horrible people and have seen people do heinous shit. But after everything that had happened, I hadn't really expected my father to think of this long running vendetta against everyone I valued in my life. My anger grew at the thought of all the trauma and pain that my father inflicted on my family and me. I wish I could have saved Hayley and my mother, because even though I had no definite proof about my mom, if she had to live with him for all of the years they were married before her death, there is a strong chance that he put her through hell. I was determined that tonight would be about starting the process in finding closure whether Neil Cross liked it or not.

The tension in my shoulders increased as my thoughts swung from one extreme to another. What I couldn't understand was why he would do all of this? What did any of this prove? Based on what Uncle Martin had said and what I'd seen as a teenager, he'd been given numerous chances to prove himself and instead of doing that, he'd chosen to destroy everything he could get his hands on, including human life.

Being in the same room as my father again had been a long time coming. I'd brought Ace with me although Lionel wanted me to come by myself.

Something about this didn't sit right with me. It all seemed to be too easy, and it was all falling into place rather neater than I thought it would. I pulled out my gun from its holster and double-checked it, making sure that it was ready to fire if needed.

I debated sending a quick message to Damien, alerting him about what was going on. It was getting late and while my team knew what was going on, someone from my family should know as well.

Me: *Damien, Lionel set up a meeting with Neil and me. It might be a trap, but I'm prepared if it is. I brought Ace along with me.*

I turned my phone on silent and looked out of the window to see if there was any activity around us. But there was nothing outside of the woods that seemed to go on for miles. I looked at the time and waited for it to reach the top of the hour when I was supposed to see my father for the first time in years.

"Do you have everything you need?"

"I do."

"I can walk to the house with you."

"Ace, you know the deal. You're to serve as backup. I don't trust these fuckers as far as I can throw them, so I wouldn't put it past them to pull something."

He nodded and I stepped out of the SUV. Ace followed suit and switched places with me, moving into the driver's seat in case we had to make a quick getaway.

As I walked up to the house, the uneasy feeling continued. I was on heightened alert because I didn't know what kind of shit my father would pull given the opportunity to kill me. I heard what sounded like a branch cracking in the distance, so I raised my gun. But I didn't see anything.

I took another step to the front door of what might be the place where all of this would end. Before I could get to the porch I saw a thin wire blocking the stairs. Someone who might not have been looking out for such a thing might have missed it, but I was prepared for any sort of trap that might have been thrown my way. Lo and behold there was one.

So his plan had been to blow me up, but he didn't have the courage to do it himself. Typical.

"You son of a—" My mumbling stopped as I quickly turned around to survey my surroundings. Lionel was a dead man once I got out of this. I heard something move in the bushes several feet to my left. I looked around again for anything else that might lead to an explosion, and when I didn't see anything, I took off. The figure behind the bush started running too, and I immediately recognized Neil's partner. The asshole was waiting to see if I tripped over that wire so that he could report back to my father. It didn't take much for me to catch him due to him being older and in not as good of shape as I was. I tackled him to the ground. I quickly stood up and turned him over. Before he was looking up at me he swung first, hitting me in the jaw, but I quickly recovered and punched him in the eye.

"Do you think this is a fucking game?" I shouted as I hit him. I only felt somewhat satisfied when my fist connected with his nose, and I heard the crunch.

"Stop! Stop!" he yelled as his hands immediately went to his nose, trying to protect himself from the blows.

"Did you think he would save you? Did you think he gave a fuck about you?" I screamed as I kicked him again. The man on the ground writhed in pain. "I made a promise to myself that I would blow your face off if you deceived me. And I have no problem carrying it out."

He shook his head fast, so hard that I thought his head might fall off his shoulders. He'd wish it had.

"So what did you do? Try to set a house on fire with me trapped inside, much like Vincent tried to do to Damien. You couldn't even be fucking original!"

I kicked him in the torso again, hoping I at the very least broke his ribs. I held my gun to his head and asked, "Is he even here? Is he watching us right now or did he send you here to do his dirty work and is waiting for you to report back?"

"I'm not telling you anything else."

"Where is he, Lionel? Is he in the city right now?"

"You tell me."

I cocked my gun at him, having mentally decided that he wasn't going to give up any more information about my father's whereabouts to me.

"You know what? You're not that different from your old man."

I shrugged. "Guess not."

I pulled the trigger and the sound that came from my gun echoed around me.

22

ELLIE

"Have you heard from him?" I asked for what felt like the millionth time.

All Damien did was shake his head.

"Ellie, I promise everything's going to be okay. Kingston is fine."

Anais's words weren't doing much to reassure me. Instead, I kept pacing, hoping that this means of relieving the tension within me would work. When I walked past my couch for what felt like the one hundredth time, I found myself staring at one of the shelves of my bookcase. Something there had caught my eye. I walked over to it, pushed one of the books to the side, and picked up the object that somewhat concealed it.

It was a small, gold figurine of a princess. From the veil on her head to the long gown she was wearing, everything about her screamed royalty. Kingston had to have put it there because he was the only one who called me that and I didn't buy it for myself. I couldn't help but smile, because it was as if Kingston had been thinking of me when he bought it and put it there. Although I found the nickname annoying before, the sentimental value of this gesture warmed my heart. I wondered why he hadn't told me about it.

"Hey Anais," I said as a happy tear slid down my face.

"What's up?"

"I think Kingston bought me this," I said with a grin. Anais walked over to me to take a look at it. That was when I noticed something dark sitting in the princess's necklace.

"What the heck is this?" I asked, not really expecting an answer from anyone in the room.

Anais leaned down to get a closer look at what I was talking about. "It almost looks like some sort of lens."

I heard Damien groan and mumble under his breath as he walked over to us, but before I could ask him what that was all about, my front door opened, and Kingston walked in.

I could see splattering of blood on his clothes, but based on my quick assessment, it didn't look to be his. What had he done?

A myriad of emotions passed over his face in the span of a few seconds, but the shocked look stayed the longest until he composed himself, hiding his true feelings from the world once more. Instead of focusing on me, Kingston's gaze was on what I was holding. "Ellie, I can explain."

"Well, you better get to talkin' then because I don't think this is a present anymore."

I heard Damien mumble again, and he shook his head. "We're going to go up to the penthouse so that you guys can chat. We're staying the night if either of you need anything."

Anais nodded and gave me a small smile before she slid her hand into his and they left my apartment.

"What is this?" I asked slowly, putting an emphasis on each word. "Why is this in my apartment? Don't lie to me."

"It's a camera."

"It's a what? You've got to be kidding me."

I thought back to how Kingston always seemed to know where I was. How he seemed to know certain things about me, things that I wasn't sure I'd shared with anyone. I chalked it up to him being observant and running a security company, but I was wrong.

"How fucking dare you. You've been stalking me!"

"Ellie, I swear it wasn't like that."

"Well, how else would you explain putting a camera in my apartment, then? Because that's what it sounds like."

"I did it for your safety."

"Without me knowing about it? How's that for my protection? How long have the cameras been in here?"

"Ellie—"

"Don't Ellie me. How long have the cameras been in here? Since before you moved in?"

Kingston nodded his head, wisely choosing not to say my name again.

"So how were they for my protection if they were in here before we knew that someone was coming to hurt me?"

I knew I had him there based on the look on his face. His head dipped slightly and then he said, "Because I wanted to be a part of your life, by any means possible. I thought you wouldn't let me in otherwise, so I did it."

His words hit me in a way I wasn't expecting, but I couldn't see past him installing cameras in my home without my permission. "Are there any other cameras in here?" The look on his face told me there were. "I want you to show me where they are and remove them."

The feelings of relief that I had when I saw him walk through the door were long gone. Now all I could see was red. When he walked past me and headed to my bedroom I felt as if I could scream. Of course he'd put a camera in my bedroom, and he probably watched me while I was undressing and sleeping. He picked up a small camera off of one of the floating shelves I'd hung up on the wall when I first moved in.

I shook my head in disgust. "Is that all?" I asked. He didn't say anything as he walked past me once more and into the kitchen and retrieved one that he had hidden between the microwave and the wall.

"Just another place I would have never checked for a camera. I hope you know that I don't feel safe in this apartment anymore. Remember when I told you that the only thing I really wanted was to feel safe at home? You ruined that!" I paused to take a deep breath because I could feel myself growing hot with anger. "What else are you hiding from me?"

My lips trembled as I took him in. I thought about asking about the blood splatter on his clothes but there were more pressing matters I had to deal with.

"It's not mine."

"I figured as much."

"Someone crossed me when I was trying to hunt down the person who wanted to hurt you. And I murdered them."

He said this without a hint of emotion, and it chilled me to the bone. The loss of human life was traumatic, and he acted as if he'd just gone for a light jog around the block. Who was this man?

"I know who is trying to hurt you. Because they are doing it to get back at me."

I didn't think I had it in me to be any more surprised anymore, but that nearly floored me. "Are you serious? Who is it?"

"My father."

My mouth dropped open as the hits kept coming. "What do I have to do with your father? I don't know the man. And how do I know you're not lying about this?"

"He knows I took an interest in you. I assume he'd had someone trailing me or my team and was able to piece it together. As a result, he decided that this was an excellent way to attack me again."

"What do you mean 'again'? A-are you referring to Hayley?"

He nodded. "I never thought her death was an accident. And possibly my mother's too because I don't trust the bastard."

"And I don't trust you."

Kingston was known for keeping his feelings under lock and key, but I could see how my words affected him. But I didn't care. I was too angry to worry about anyone else's feelings but my own. "I feel violated in my own apartment."

"That isn't how I wanted to make you feel."

"Well, you failed. Now get your things and get out."

"Ellie—"

I shook my head. "Stop. Gather your things, including whatever you used to watch me, and leave."

I could see that he wanted to argue with me, but my answer was final. No, I didn't know what I was going to do about Kingston's father following me, but there was no way that I was going to allow a liar to stay in my presence. I trusted him to keep me safe, but all he did was break my spirit.

Before he opened my front door, he turned to me and said, "Just because I took those cameras down, Ellie, doesn't mean I'm not watching you. I promised to keep you safe and that's what I'm going to do."

He didn't wait for me to respond before he left. When my front door closed behind him, I couldn't hold any of my tears back, without fear of him noticing how much he hurt me.

A small knock on the door made me jump, and before I could bring my hands to my face to wipe my tears, Anais entered. As soon as she saw me, she pulled me into her arms and held me without saying another word.

23

KINGSTON

I watched Damien as he handed me a finger of whiskey and sat down across from me. He raised his glass and I followed suit before we both took a sip.

It had been about a week since the fiasco with Lionel and my confession to Ellie, and I'd been in a shitty place ever since. I missed her with everything in me, and I didn't know if I would ever come back from this.

After Hayley died, I didn't care about finding someone who I enjoyed spending time with outside of my friends and family. I'd closed myself off to the possibility and over the last week I was finally able to label why I'd done it. It was all out of fear. Fear of losing again. And yet here I was, having lost again, not in the same way, but the pain was still there.

"You know you were wrong for putting those cameras up in her place, right?"

"Hadn't figured that out yet," I said sarcastically. I sighed and ran a hand through my hair. "My intention was only to protect her."

"Stop lying to yourself."

I kept my face blank, instead choosing to focus on the drink in my hand. I wasn't necessarily lying to myself, but I was lying to the world. The reason why I installed the cameras in her home was for myself, to feel as if I were a part of her life when I knew there was no way she would let me in due to how much she hated me at the time. Then I manipulated the situation to my benefit once I found out about my father targeting her.

Would I have done things differently? No, but I understood where she was coming from and felt terrible about making her feel that way.

"You're right—"

Damien interrupted me before I could finish. "You don't say that all that often."

"You know what I mean. I didn't just put the cameras up to protect her. I wanted to be with her before I realized I did. It started off with us running into each other due to our social circle, yet she hated my guts, and then it blossomed into something completely...unexpected. And it seems as if we've come full circle because she's pissed at me all over again."

"In addition to being in danger again because of her association with you. Have you heard from Neil?"

I shook my head. "I'm still pissed at what Lionel pulled. None of my team have been able to trace anything related to Neil, so the only link we had to him is now dead. I made a mistake in killing him. Fuck."

"I heard from Will."

I sat up and leaned forward, my eyes focused on Damien. "And?"

"He knows about Neil and how he influenced and helped Vincent with all of his shit against our family and the harm he caused Charlotte. He's after him and if he finds him first..."

Then I wouldn't have a chance to kill my father. I was pretty sure that Will would have no problem delivering the body to my doorstep, much like what had happened when Damien delivered Vincent's to Will.

"Are you still watching Ellie?"

"In her home? No. I removed the cameras, but there was no way in hell I wasn't keeping eyes on her in case Neil showed up."

"You love her." Before I could protest, he continued. "You don't have to admit it out loud. Trust me, having been in a very similar situation with Anais, I can see it and it doesn't do you any good in lying to yourself about that either."

This time I rolled my eyes. When had Damien gotten so preachy?

"Are you done?"

"About that? Sure, but there's one thing I wanted to ask."

"Have at it."

"Are you ready to pull the trigger if need be on Neil?"

I could see what he was getting at. Murdering your father wasn't something one chose to do on a regular basis, and the ramifications that it would have on me were in the back of my mind.

I took another sip from my drink before I replied. "If it meant saving her life? Absolutely."

"And you know he's probably not going to stop until he hurts her. Because it would mean that he succeeded in hurting you."

"I understand that. I will not hesitate to end that fucker's life if it means saving hers. You have my word."

24

ELLIE

I sniffled again. Although the tears had stopped, my sadness remained at the state that my life was currently in. I couldn't process where things had gone so horribly wrong, yet here I was lying on my couch with my best friend sitting next to my head and in somewhat of a daze about the shitshow that was currently my life.

Anais tried her best to comfort me and we both settled on us sitting quietly while a television show played in the background. What was happening in the episode? I had no clue. There was no way that I could pay attention to what was happening on the screen during a time like this.

"This has completely rocked me," I said. That was the truth. After the showdown with Kingston, I hadn't gotten much sleep, which had not made things easier on me when it came to doing my job. The weight on my mind based on the circumstances was taking its toll. I missed him. I missed sleeping next to him, forcing him to watch marathons of some of my favorite shows that he'd never seen and spending time with him. He'd become such an intricate part of my daily life, that him not being around felt like a huge loss.

Yet, I was devastated about what he had done.

"I know and I bet you never would have thought you would feel this way."

I nodded and sniffled again. "I've been torn down about relationship shit before, but not like this."

"It's a lot to take in. Not only are you dealing with being in a dangerous situation, but the person who has been closest to you for the last few weeks has completely betrayed you. It's not a surprise that you're feeling the way you do. If you weren't, I might be worried."

Anais's reassurance that I wasn't overreacting made me feel a little bit better.

"That's because you fell in love with him."

And then she had to drop that bomb on me. I lifted my head slightly to look at her, but the strength it took to hold it up felt like too much, so my head dropped back down on the cushion.

I couldn't deny it. I tried to form an argument, but I came up short. "You're absolutely right."

"It's going to be okay, no matter what happens."

"I know, but it doesn't feel that way right now. I need to focus on making sure that Kingston's father doesn't kill me."

"There's also the slight chance that he might have backed off if he knows that you and Kingston are on the outs."

When I looked up at Anais again, she raised her hands up. "It was just a suggestion."

"Yeah, that we both know isn't true. Especially if he's anything like Kingston."

"Is there anything I can do?"

"I don't know. It feels somewhat weird continuing life without him around. I also don't have anyone watching me anymore, so I need to be better prepared if Neil tries something. I think I still have my mace..."

Anais bit the corner of her lip but said nothing.

"What are you thinking about?"

"Nothing."

"Sure doesn't look like nothing."

"I was trying to think of what else we could do, but I'm not sure what outside of Kingston's organization or sending you away until he's caught, what we should do."

I shook my head. "I'm not going into hiding. I refuse. Not again."

"Well then we should make sure that you're as prepared as possible to face him."

25

ELLIE

A sudden sound startled me as I was cleaning up after I'd walked out my last client for the day.

"Jill?" I called out, hoping it was her, but I heard nothing in response. Goosebumps appeared on my arms as I grew concerned because she should have been able to hear me from the front desk. Maybe she'd gone to the bathroom?

When I heard another loud crash, my mind wanted me to run out of the building to the back exit.

I bent down quietly and grabbed my mace from my purse. At the same time, I managed to call Kingston's cell phone and put my phone back in my pocket in hopes that if he did answer, he might be able to hear what was going on. This was more than likely unnecessary, but I had no problem giving into my paranoia in hopes that I was overreacting. I looked to see if there was another weapon I could grab on the way down the hall but came up empty-handed.

Now I wished I had that princess figurine that Kingston

had stashed in my apartment. At least with that, he would have been alerted to what was currently going on at the spa.

I walked toward the waiting area and found Jill standing up straight with her eyes wide and her mouth trembling.

"Where is she?"

Fuck. It was only a matter of time before either one of them spotted me.

As if she heard me, Jill looked my way, probably seeing something out of the corner of her eye, before her head snapped back to look straight ahead. Then I heard a dark chuckle before someone spoke.

"Nice of you to join us, Ellie. I was looking for you."

With a deep breath, I walked out of my hiding space and came face-to-face with Neil Cross. I'd seen pictures of him when I'd done some research on Kingston and the Cross family, but all that I could find was older pictures. Kingston favored his father greatly, but the elder Cross looked older than his age, as if he'd come across harder times in recent years.

"Come here, we have places to go and things to do. I don't want to have to hurt Jill to prove a point about what I can do to you."

I walked toward him with my hand resting on the item that might get both Jill and me out of here unscathed. I spared her a glance as I walked by, hoping that my being there now provided some reassurance for her because I was tossing together an idea that might either be the smartest thing I ever did or the dumbest.

"Promise me if I come with you that you'll leave Jill alone."

Neil Cross stared at me before using the barrel of the gun

to sweep some of my hair that had fallen out of my ponytail out of my face.

"You know, I can see why my son took an interest in you."

His words and the meaning behind them disgusted me more than I could have ever thought. The way he looked at me made me think that he was undressing me with his eyes and that there was no way that I could leave this building with him. If I did, I was more than likely signing my death certificate. I needed to act fast.

I whipped the mace out of my pocket and without thinking sprayed him in the eyes. He hadn't been expecting it and I used my body weight to get the gun out of his hand. When slammed to the ground, I scrambled to grab it before standing up.

My hand shook as I held the gun out in front of me. Was I aiming this thing properly? Was there a safety on? Of course, since I'd never held a gun before, I had no idea what I was doing but this was a matter of life or death. I swallowed hard as I stared at the man in front of me and prayed that no matter what he did, I would be able to counteract it.

"Ellie, don't."

I glanced out of the corner of my eye, determined not to fully take my attention off of the man in front of me. Kingston walked into the waiting area from what I assumed was the exit near the back of the spa and appeared next to me. He placed a hand on the gun I was holding and lowered it before taking it.

I looked at Kingston in confusion. "You're here! You must have gotten my call... What are you doing?"

Neil smirked and I could see the resemblance between the two. "Being smart for the first time in his life."

His harsh words gave me an insight on how he must have treated Kingston as a child. He practically sneered at his only child, his flesh and blood. Even though I was still hurt by Kingston's behavior toward me, I still felt for him and what kind of hell his childhood must have been.

My distraction was an opportunity because Neil whipped out another gun and pointed it at me. Kingston took the gun I'd given him and held it up so that Neil was the intended target.

Neil turned to Jill and said, "I have no use for you anymore. You may leave."

Jill looked stunned for a moment, before she rushed out of the building. I hoped she would be able to call the police and get someone here quickly.

"You know I would have done it again."

"Done what?" Kingston asked, his face as hard as stone.

I could only imagine what it felt like to be on the brink of killing your father.

"Kill the most important people in your life."

I gasped at his father seemingly admitting to killing not only Kingston's mother but his wife too. Kingston tightened his grip on the gun, and it didn't take much to see that he was debating his next move. Whether or not he should be the one to take his father's life.

"Why'd you do it?" Kingston's words were void of any emotion. Frankly, it frightened me more than if he'd been screaming at Neil.

Neil's lips formed a smile, much like the one I'd seen appear on his son's face except this was much more sinister. The difference between the two men in the room couldn't be more apparent. "Your mother was in love with my brother."

No one, but Neil moved an inch.

"You're such a liar. Mom loved you with everything in her until she died."

Neil slowly shook his head. "No, she loved the lifestyle I was able to provide her with after she couldn't land Martin. It had gotten to the point where I wondered if they were fucking behind my back and then she became pregnant with you."

My mouth opened slightly at the information that Neil had no problem now telling his only child.

"We'd tried to get pregnant for a couple of years before you were conceived. Then Martin stayed with us for one weekend and a few weeks later your mother was pregnant with you."

My eyes jumped back and forth between the two men, wondering what he was going to say next.

"Uncle Martin being my father is irrelevant because he was still a way better father figure than you ever were."

Neil's face switched from a smirk into a nasty snarl. "Shut the fuck up. I made sure that you were my kid. Did nothing to lessen the hate I had for Martin or your mother."

"And as a result, you then hated me."

Neil's lips twitched. "I didn't hate you. I hoped with your mother out of the picture, we could spend more time together and then Martin opened his doors to you and gave you the option of living with him. And you chose to do so. You know he threatened that he would end me if I ever tried to fight him on it. He tossed quite a bit of money at me so I would stay quiet about it, at least until you were eighteen and could make your own decisions."

"Because he knows you're an asshole that has no business raising a child."

"That mouth is all your mother's and it served her until the bitter end. She mentioned that she should have married Martin during a fight with me...it so happens to be the last words she ever spoke."

Kingston made a move as if he was going to charge at his father, but Neil pointed the gun at him before putting it back to my head. "You know I have no problem killing her. She's worthless to me and I know she means everything to you."

Kingston glared at his father but didn't try to come at him again.

"Martin took my son from me and so I was determined to take at least one of his. I failed in that regard, but I succeeded in killing Hayley, which was one of my finer achievements if I do say so myself."

This time, Kingston's face remained stoic, as if he was letting the words roll off his back, but I knew it had to hurt. At least he was finding out what actually happened to his loved ones, and I hope it would bring him some peace.

"But you had to fall in love again and bring another woman into your shitty life. Well, if it's the last thing I do, I'm happy to make sure she joins me in hell."

I watched as Kingston's eyes shifted slightly, but he didn't move a muscle.

"You can't even pull the trigger. You're weak, just like your mother."

I could see that Neil's hand had tightened on the gun and then a shot rang out. I screamed. My hands flew up to my ears, although it was too late. My ears were ringing, and my heart was pounding as I tried to process what I had seen.

Before I could do anything else, I was pulled against something hard, yet warm.

"Keep your eyes closed and focus on me, okay?"

I nodded and quickly understood what he was trying to do. It was as if he was trying to shield me from what I assumed was a very gruesome sight.

Kingston looked over behind him and I followed suit. I could see a hole almost directly behind me. "He tried to shoot me!"

"And thankfully I'm a better shot. I should have done that years ago when I had the chance. Maybe I could have saved everyone from this pain."

I could hear Neil groaning on the floor, but I refused to look, instead choosing to listen to Kingston's fast beating heart "Don't you dare blame yourself for any of this. How could you have known?"

"Because... because I'm just like him."

"No. You're not." I pulled Kingston toward me and put my hands on his cheeks. The years of hurt and pain couldn't be masked on his face. "You care about people, especially those that you view as being a part of your family. Whether they are related by blood or not. Neil only gave a shit about himself and the revenge he wanted to enact. You're nothing like that."

Kingston didn't respond, but when he pulled me into his arms and tightened his grip, I knew he'd heard me. He hadn't shut me out.

When his eyes glazed over and hardened, I knew that my initial assessment had been wrong. He'd put his emotions behind this mask as if we were strangers once again.

"I promised you that I would keep you safe and I fulfilled that obligation."

"I know and I was hoping that we could talk about—"

"Ellie!" I turned and found Anais and Grace sprinting toward me with Damien and Broderick just steps behind them. I hugged Anais, while Grace began checking me out to see if I was okay. When I turned around to see where Kingston went, he was nowhere to be found, having seemingly vanished into thin air.

26

KINGSTON

I knocked on the door and waited for a response to go inside. While I waited, I looked down and saw a message from Ellie. I wanted to respond to her, to tell her everything I'd been thinking about and beg for forgiveness, but I couldn't. Something was holding me back from replying and I hadn't been able to label it. Yes, with my father out of the picture, a burden had been lifted off of all of our shoulders, but something still didn't sit right with me so I hoped that this would put me on the path to feeling something more than the despair I had been feeling.

At least it was a change from the life I'd been living previously, although not completely for the better.

"Come in."

I did as instructed, and found Uncle Martin sitting, once again, behind his big wooden desk. He placed the phone down on the receiver and gestured for me to enter the room. While I closed the door behind me, he stood up and walked over to me. Instead of saying something, he pulled me into his arms and held me, reminding me of how Aunt Selena would have done the same if she were present.

When I took a step back after who knew how long, he looked at me and said, "I didn't hug you boys nearly enough when you were children so I know that must have been weird. I'm so sorry you had to do that. If I would have known, I—"

"How could you have known? Neil had so many problems that he—"

"But it shouldn't be something you have to bear. I would have rather it been me that pulled the trigger."

Of course he would have. Because he cares about his family.

"Neil said... He said you and Mom had an affair. He thought I might be your son and he made sure that wasn't the case. I assume that meant that he had a paternity test done. He was pissed when you took me in and treated me like yours after he murdered Mom."

I watched his face as I spoke, and he looked appalled at the idea. When I finished, he leaned forward in his chair. "Your mother and I never had an affair. I swear on everything because I would never do that to my family. When I was at their place for the weekend, I went on several dates with Selena and was trying to convince her to date me. That took more time than I'll ever be willing to admit let alone getting her to marry me."

I believed him. I'd always known Uncle Martin to be an honest man and why would that change now?

"Now what should I do? I feel free from him because he's dead, but he's stolen so much from me that I still feel his presence everywhere."

"Take it one day at a time. Get away if you need to. Take

time for yourself and truly think about how you can get past this. Talk to a therapist about it. Much like how you took care of your guys when Neil had Sawyer killed."

"How did you—"

"I have eyes and ears everywhere much like you do."

"Okay, I'm going to get out of the city for a bit."

"Where are you going?"

I shrugged. "Not sure yet, but I'll be back soon. Thanks for everything."

With that, I left Uncle Martin's place and stepped out into the cool breeze that had settled in New York City. Where this newfound freedom would take me, I had no idea.

27

ELLIE
FOUR WEEKS LATER

It had been four weeks since I'd last seen Kingston. I tried calling him, texting him, emailing him, but it was as if the man had fallen off of the face of the Earth.

I'd even stopped by his place and one of his neighbors had said he moved out weeks ago, almost around the same time he'd saved me from his father.

Neil Cross died at the hospital from a gunshot wound to the chest. I couldn't imagine what type of courage it took to kill your parent, but Kingston had done so to save my life and potentially his own. Neil didn't know that Kingston had brought the princess figurine with him and had recorded the entire conversation. As heinous as the events that happened in Devotional Spa were, I hoped that it brought Kingston some closure.

"Miss, do you want me to wait for you?"

I shook my head. "No, thank you," I said bravely even though I didn't feel that way. I was taking a huge risk by being here, and I didn't know what the result would be.

After I paid the driver, I stepped out of the taxi,

smoothing my black dress down after I closed the door. It wasn't difficult to spot Kingston because he was the only person in this area as far as I could see.

I felt guilty for coming to see him while he was visiting the graves of his mother and wife, but it was the only option I had.

The taxi drove away, but I didn't move from where I stood, hoping to give Kingston the space and time that he needed.

"Damien told me where to find you because you've been a hard man to track down. When you want to disappear you really disappear. I—I didn't want to disturb you, but you wouldn't answer your phone and I had no way to contact you."

"So you stalked me."

For the first time in what felt like forever, I laughed. It felt amazing and further cemented how much I'd missed him.

"Ellie, I want to apologize for deceiving you. I should have been upfront about what I'd done or just hadn't done it at all. I genuinely wanted to be a part of your life in any way I could and thought that it was the best possible way at the time. Then it became an option to help with protecting you."

I took a deep breath and said, "If I'm being honest, I understand the latter, but not the former. I'd appreciate it if you talked to me instead of acting, especially when something affects me and my life directly."

"I'll try."

I snorted because of course he would say that.

"There's something else I need to get off my chest. Ellie, I'm in love with you."

I couldn't control the gasp that fled my body. I knew that I loved him, but I hadn't been expecting him to tell me right then and there.

"I love you too, Kingston."

I meant those words from the bottom of my heart.

"I have one more thing I need to do. A promise that I made needs to be fulfilled. There are some people I want you to meet."

Confusion muddled my brain as I looked around, confirming that there was still no one here. Kingston walked me over to the tombstones that lay side by side. He kneeled and I followed suit the best I could in my dress.

"Long ago I made the promise to my mother and Hayley that I would bring the woman that I fell in love with to meet them."

Tears streamed down my face, and I didn't bother to hide them. I was done hiding how I felt about anything including how I felt about him. Instead, he turned to me and wiped the tears, and I smiled at his thoughtfulness. I swooned when I got a genuine smile in return.

Kingston turned back to the tombstones and said, "Mom and Hayley, I want you to meet Ellie."

EPILOGUE

KINGSTON

"Do we have to watch this again?"

I snorted. This was coming from someone who would have done anything to find someone to binge-watch this show with. Now, it was a problem.

Staying with Ellie this time around, proved to be a treasure. Although we hadn't officially moved in together, I found myself staying at her apartment more and more although the threat to her life had been eradicated. I was in the process of making her dreams come true and had been searching for a home to live in that would allow us to be closer to her parents and I couldn't wait to surprise her with it.

"You love this show, Princess."

Ellie glanced at me. "But now you love it and it's weird. And you never explained why you called me that."

"When you were arguing with me in front of the basement door of Elevate, you reminded of the exact opposite of what royalty was supposed to act like and then when we were forced to be around each other more frequently, I loved your fierce loyalty to Anais even if you kept busting my balls every chance you got. I guess you were loyal to that in a way. Also I had a feeling it would probably annoy you, so the nickname stuck." I paused as another thought crossed my mind. "Thinking about you in the dress you wore the first time we met has me hard."

"Good enough I guess. Now what's this you say about being hard?"

I chuckled and leant down to kiss her, hoping that it would turn into something more before my phone rang. I groaned as I picked the device up and this time it was Ellie's turn to chuckle. The number that flashed on my screen somewhat surprised me.

"Hey."

"I'm outside your girl's building. We need to talk."

Usually I was the one to go to Ace with things, not the other way around. In fact, I had something I wanted to share with him, but was going to reach out in a couple of days.

"I'll let the front desk know so that you can come up."

Ace hung up and I turned to fill Ellie in on what had just occurred. As I was standing up, we heard a knock on the door. Ellie nodded and I opened the door to find Ace on the other side.

Ellie placed her hand on my shoulder, and I looked down at her. "I'm going to call Anais in my bedroom to talk over some of her plans for the wedding. It's nice seeing you again, Ace."

"Likewise."

Ellie leaned over and kissed me on the lips, not caring that Ace was standing in front of us. She then walked into the bedroom. I backed up and let Ace enter the apartment and we both sat down on the couch that Ellie and I had occupied.

"You look very happy."

His observation made me smile. "I am. But you know what would make me happier?"

Ace raised an eyebrow.

"When you decide that you are finally going to join me at Cross Sentinel. We work on enough cases together, so it only makes sense."

"When pigs fly."

I shook my head. I had a feeling that that would be his answer. "Well, I do have another case for you."

Instead of saying something, Ace held out his hand and I placed the manila file in it.

"You want me to go and see what I can find out about the case that Will gave you."

"Yes. You're going to attend a party for them at one of their mansions upstate. Feel free to use your real name because it will probably open more doors here than it has in the past, if you know what I mean." Ace nodded showing that he understood what I meant. "He thinks that some funny shit might be occurring."

Ace raised an eyebrow at me. "What type of party?"

"We don't know, everyone who's attended has kept their mouths shut and all the digging I've done hasn't gotten us far. But there is something off about them and he wants to know what and why. Read through the file." I gestured to the folder in his hand. Ace flipped the folder open. His face remained stoic as he read through the file.

When he didn't respond, I said, "Ever been to a party with these people?"

"Nope. They wouldn't have allowed someone like me in before."

I knew he was referring to the lack of money he had in previous years. "But now they will."

He stared at me for a moment and then gave me a nod as he put the file in the bag he brought with him. To my surprise he pulled out a file, identical to the one I gave him and tossed it on my desk.

"What is this?"

"You're not the only one who has files. Open it."

I did as he said and quickly scanned the pages.

"Who is Raven Goodwin?"

"Keep reading."

I read another section. "How accurate is this?"

"Most of the information in it I verified myself."

I ran my finger down the information in the file, taking everything in.

"This can't be right."

"I promise you it is."

"According to this, I have a half-sister... There's another Cross out there that we knew nothing about."

Ace remained quiet. Probably because I was talking to myself versus talking to him.

"What are the odds that she would be attending Brentson University right now? That can't be a coincidence," I mumbled as I kept the information in front of me.

"I didn't think it was either."

I flipped one of the pages back and forth before looking up at Ace. "Something's missing."

"What's that?"

"Why did she leave Brentson and what happened in the years before she went back?"

Ace clasped his hands together in front of him. "That, I

have no idea. But what I do know is that she needs your help."

∽

THANK you for reading Stolen Empire! Although Ellie and Kingston's story completes the Broken Cross series, you will see them and the rest of the Cross family in my new stories, The Billionaire's Auction and Devious Game. Keep reading to find a sneak peek of them!

DON'T WANT to let Kingston and Ellie go just yet? Click HERE to grab a bonus scene featuring the couple!

WANT to join discussions about the Broken Cross Series? Click HERE to join my Reader Group on Facebook.

PLEASE JOIN my newsletter to find out the latest about the Broken Cross series and my other books!

THE BILLIONAIRE'S AUCTION BLURB

Desperate times lead to desperate measures...

That's why I did the auction.
   The money from it would be my way out.
   My last chance.
   Then I saw him, and hope flashed through my mind when he placed a bid.
   It shouldn't have.
   Because I didn't know about the dark edges that surrounded his soul, the ones that should never see the light of day.
   Now I'm tied to him for ninety days, but I can survive this.
   I've been through so much worse before.
   Or so I thought.
   Because my hope? Was nothing more than a façade.
   Now, he was my monster.

SNEAK PEEK OF THE BILLIONAIRE'S AUCTION

Fucking assholes everywhere.

That was the perfect word to describe people in the home I'd just entered. I hated these types of people, the arrogant assholes who didn't give a damn about anyone else, but I could deal with it for the time being because I had only one thing on my mind: gathering as much intel as I could to take back to Kingston.

Why he was involved in this was beyond me, but that was neither here nor there.

I walked past two men who were sitting in two chairs next to one another. Both sized me up as I walked past, and one even had the audacity to suck on his cigar and attempt to send a billow of smoke my way. My inclination was to have a little chat with him, but I refused to let the asshole shift my focus. There would be a time and place to deal with him later.

"Mr. Bolton."

I turned to face the person who had called my name. I

didn't use an alternative identity when I requested an invitation to this event.

I raised an eyebrow at the young woman standing in front of me. It was interesting that she knew who I was because I hadn't submitted a picture to go along with my request. So who here was keeping tabs on me? I could hazard a guess if she worked for who I thought she did.

"Follow me and I'll show you to your seat."

I spared one last glance at the two men before following the woman through a set of doors that opened up into a larger sitting area. The living space was organized with a makeshift stage near a set of windows with the blinds drawn. Chairs were lined up on the opposite side, ready for everyone to see what would be occurring on the stage in front. People were milling around and as we walked by, the young woman whose name I never caught gently told them that the show would be starting soon.

"Here's your seat, Mr. Bolton. I hope you enjoy your time here tonight."

I looked at her for a moment before I took my seat. *What the hell has Kingston gotten me into?*

A survey of the room didn't give me much insight into what was going on. People were chit-chatting with one another, and I seemed to be the only one who didn't have anyone to talk to. Which was how I preferred it.

Everyone around me started making their way to their seats, and I looked down at my phone. I found Kingston's phone number and sent him a text message.

Me: *What the hell is this all about?*

Before I could get a response, I could hear the murmurs getting lower and I wondered what had caused it. When I looked up, I found a man in a suit who looked as if he'd thrown it on in a hurry. Next to him stood a woman who immediately took my breath away.

That was until I saw her face. When our eyes met, I saw fear shining in hers.

The man next to her cleared his throat and said, "Who's ready to bid on this lovely woman in red?"

The Billionaire's Auction is available for pre-order and will be released in 2022.

DEVIOUS GAME BLURB

I left this town in the dead of night three years ago, promising never to return.

Brentson was supposed to be a thing of the past, but here's the thing about the past:

It always has a screwed-up way of hunting you down.

Now, I'm face-to-face with Nash Henson, my ex-boyfriend and crowned king of Brentson University.

He'll never forgive me for what I've done.

And when he's done playing his games with me, I'm not sure there'll be anything left because he's determined to destroy me.

SNEAK PEEK OF DEVIOUS GAME

My hand tightened on the steering wheel as I drove past a familiar sign.

Welcome to Brentson

The elaborate sign was meant to offer a warm embrace and show Brentson's hospitality. Except I felt anything but welcomed.

The only thing keeping me calm was the cool breeze that felt like a gentle whisper on my face as I drove through Brentson. Late August into early September was always one of my favorite times in the town. With the leaves already starting to change, it painted a pretty picture of my hometown. What should have been a time to bask in remembering the good times I spent here was anything but. I spent many afternoons during high school at Smith's Ice Cream Parlor—still standing and as popular as ever. Many of my memories there included Nash Henson, someone I tried to forget over the years. And I failed every single time.

A few minutes later, and with a heavy sigh, I steered my old Toyota Camry onto Brentson University's campus. Another welcome sign beaconed me home. Butterflies collided in my stomach as I took in my surroundings. What once had been my dream school was now my living nightmare. As a kid, I'd hoped that I would one day enroll at BU. Now that I had the opportunity, it felt as if hell had swallowed me whole.

Transferring to Brentson had been a lot simpler than I thought it would be, and for that I was grateful. Not having to deal with that on top of everything else was crucial in helping me prepare for this move across the country.

I looked at the map on my phone before turning off the GPS. I knew where I was now. Some things had changed in the last three years, but most of what I remembered about this town had stayed the same. Recalling the last couple of directions from the GPS, I navigated to a small home and pulled into the driveway. It looked well maintained, which wasn't surprising given that it was owned by the university.

Before I had an opportunity to move, the front door swung open and out popped a petite woman with a huge smile on her face.

"You're here!"

I nodded and gave her a small smile through the windshield. Seeing Izzy Deacon did nothing to calm the nerves building in my body. With a shaky hand, I stepped out of the car, locked up, and took a deep breath. She bounded down the stairs and pulled me into her arms.

It felt wonderful to be reunited with Izzy again. We had seen each other in person a couple of times over the years, but it had been months since we last hung out.

"Glad you made it here okay. I've been dying to hear more about why you decided to transfer here for our senior year."

There was only so much I could tell her because I needed to do my best to make sure that no one else would be affected by this mess. "Izzy, I'll fill you in. I promise."

That seemed to satisfy her as a smile reappeared on her face.

"We have to get you settled. You mentioned that you were having trouble finding a place and I wanted you to know that you could always stay with me. I know there is no way in hell you'd go back home."

"I appreciate the offer, but I know I'll find something near campus."

Izzy crossed her arms in a huff. "Well, you should stay with me until you do."

I shifted my weight from one foot to the other. "Okay."

"Yay!" Izzy exclaimed with childlike glee. "It's been way too long since we've spent time together. I've been waiting for this ever since you said you were coming back." Without another word, Izzy pulled me into another hug.

"I've been looking forward to this, too." That wasn't a lie. I had looked forward to spending time with Izzy since I knew I was coming back to Brentson.

"Oh, no."

Izzy whispered this in my ear because we were still hugging. It was clear that something was wrong. When her arms loosened, and I regained the ability to move, I looked over my shoulder before doing a one-eighty. Standing across the street was the last person I was ready to see again.

My breath caught in my chest when his eyes landed on me.

Nash.

He still looked as handsome as I remembered. Any hope I had that he might have forgotten all the things I did was dashed when his eyes narrowed. And he glared at me. If he could have snarled at me from where he was, he would have. He wasn't alone, and soon the guy with him drew his attention away from me. But, as he left, he gave me one final stare.

I watched him walk away, not blaming him one bit for his reaction.

My name might be Raven Goodwin, but I was far from good.

Devious Game is available for pre-order and will be released in 2022.

ABOUT THE AUTHOR

Bri loves a good romance, especially ones that involve a hot anti-hero. That is why she likes to turn the dial up a notch with her own writing. Her Broken Cross series is her debut dark romance series.

She spends most of her time hanging out with her family, plotting her next novel, or reading books by other romance authors.

briblackwood.com

ALSO BY BRI BLACKWOOD

Broken Cross Series

Sinners Empire (Prequel)

Savage Empire

Scarred Empire

Steel Empire

Shadow Empire

Secret Empire

Stolen Empire

Brentson University Series

Devious Game

The Billionaire Trilogy

The Billionaire's Auction

Made in United States
Cleveland, OH
30 December 2024